"Can't handle it, princess?"

Reilly's drawling tone shouldn't have annoyed Carlie. After all, he didn't know he was accusing Sister Mary Charles, a woman dedicated to poverty, chastity and obedience, of being a spoiled brat.

"I can handle anything you can," she snapped back. "But we happen to have a baby with us."

He turned to look down at her. "Okay, we'll rest. Half an hour. We already got a much later start than I planned. You were the one who overslept."

"You were the one who didn't wake me," she retorted, then stopped, appalled. Hadn't she learned docility and obedience?

But Reilly didn't make her feel docile or obedient. She was out in the world, among men. For the next few days, she'd give herself permission to feel anger. Fear. Tenderness. For the next few days, she might even feel love....

ABOUT THE AUTHOR

Anne Stuart likes passionate stories and tales of love that transcend the experience of everyday life. She's also more than passingly fond of her "gorgeous husband and two wonderful children, not to mention her dog and four cats." A long-time contributor to Harlequin American Romance, Anne Stuart has warmed the hearts of readers worldwide.

Books by Anne Stuart

Anne Stuart

THE SOLDIER &
THE BABY

Harlequin Books

TORONTO • NEW YORK • LONDON
AMSTERDAM • PARIS • SYDNEY • HAMBURG
STOCKHOLM • ATHENS • TOKYO • MILAN
MADRID • WARSAW • BUDAPEST • AUCKLAND

ISBN 0-373-16573-0

THE SOLDIER & THE BABY

Chapter One

She moved through the empty hallways, her sandaled feet silent beneath the heavy swish of her long skirts. It was a quiet afternoon—the jungle surrounding the decaying remains of the Convent of Our Lady of Repose was thick and heavy with heat and somnolence. Even the birds and the monkeys had lapsed into a drowsy trance.

Every living creature with sense napped during the hottest part of the day in the tiny Central American country of San Pablo. Every living creature, that is, except for Carlie Forrest, better known as Sister Maria Carlos, novice of the order of the Sisters of Benevolence. She was the only member of the religious community still trapped in that revolution-torn place.

The others had left, swiftly, safely. Most of them would be in Spain by now, Mother Superior had said, though a few would head down to Brazil, where there was a large and thriving sister house. Only Carlie had remained behind. Carlie and her patients.

"I don't like leaving you behind in this situation," Reverend Mother Ignacia had said, her wrinkled face creased with worry. "I don't like leaving anyone behind, but Sister Mary Agnes is too old and sick to travel, and Caterina's baby is already a week overdue. I don't dare risk taking either of them, and you're the only one with midwifery skills as well as medical knowledge.''

"I'll be fine," Carlie had answered with deceptive serenity. "I doubt you could make me leave."

"I haven't forgotten what brought you here to us, my child," Mother Ignacia had said gently. "I would give anything not to put you in the way of that kind of situation again."

"I survived when I was seventeen," Carlie had replied, pleating the folds of her habit. "I'm stronger now."

"I know you are," Mother Ignacia had said. "But I still would spare you if I could. I suppose I shouldn't worry—this might be just what you need. It might give you time to think a few things through. You'll be safe enough here—neither the soldiers nor the rebels would dare interfere with a convent. I'm afraid that Sister Mary Agnes hasn't long, poor old lady, but Caterina is young and strong. Once she delivers her baby her family will see to her, and you can follow us to Brazil if things haven't stabilized. And if it's still what you want. Matteo will arrange safe transport."

"It's what I want," Carlie had said quietly. "There's nothing I need to think through. I've been with the Sisters of Benevolence for nine years now, and all I've ever wanted was to take my final vows."

It was an old argument, one Mother Ignacia was skilled at countering. "When you join us in Brazil we will talk about it again."

"I'm ready, Mother," Carlie had said, allowing the note of desperation to creep in.

"I'm sure you feel that way, my child. I just can't rid myself of the notion that you are running away from life, rather than running to us."

Even now, on that still and silent afternoon, Mother Ignacia's words rang in her head. Carlie prided herself on her self-knowledge, and the fear that Reverend Mother might be right terrified her more than any human or wild beast that might roam the jungle outside the abandoned convent.

It was blistering hot, even for one who was used to it. She didn't dare go swimming—there were newcomers in the area, soldiers, people who didn't want to be seen. She hadn't yet sent word to Matteo and for very good reason.

The baby wasn't ready to travel.

Mother Ignacia had been right about one thing. Sister Mary Agnes hadn't lasted long—within three days of the emptying of the convent the old nun had breathed her last. She'd received her last rites more than a week before, and she hadn't regained consciousness. It had been a good life, a long one, serving God, and Carlie hadn't even wept when she'd laid her out.

But the Reverend Mother had been wrong about something else. Caterina Rosaria Morrissey de Mendino had delivered her baby easily enough, a small, healthy little boy she'd named William Timothy. And then she'd quietly, swiftly died.

Matteo had come to bury them. Matteo had crossed himself, muttered something about seeing to her escape, then looked askance at the newborn. "The baby will never survive," he'd said. "And just as well."

"What do you mean?" Carlie had demanded, exhaustion and shock tearing away at her fundamental calm.

"This country has had enough of the Mendinos. They have ruled San Pablo, bled it dry for the past forty years. It is better than no trace of them remain. God has chosen to take the little one's mother—if God doesn't take the baby, then the soldiers will. They, or the rebels."

"Caterina had nothing to do with her father's crimes."

"She was the daughter of the *presidente*. Her son would be of the same line."

"Son?" Carlie had said instantly. "What makes you think the child is a boy?"

Matteo had looked confused for a moment. "I thought you said..."

"Caterina gave birth to a baby girl," Carlie had said firmly. "She named her after her mother."

Matteo had crossed himself. "Poor little thing. I promised Mother Ignacia I would find a way out for you, Sister Maria Carlos. I can't promise I can find a way for the baby."

"I won't leave without... her." The hesitation had been so brief Matteo hadn't noticed.

"I will see what I can manage."

It had been three weeks. The baby had grown stronger, the supply of powdered formula and clean water had been more than sufficient, and it seemed as if everyone, including Matteo and the baby's father, had forgotten their existence.

For that Carlie would only be grateful.

It was bad enough that she was alone in the midst of a revolution-torn country, with an infant, no weapons and no disposition to use any if she were to possess them. But that baby was the only grandchild of the notorious Hector Mendino, deposed and executed dictator of San Pablo.

Hector Mendino had fathered no children. His second wife already had a daughter from her previous marriage—Caterina—and Mendino had adopted her. Caterina had always disliked her brutal stepfather, but that hadn't stopped Mendino. And it wouldn't stop the rebels, who saw any connection to Mendino as something to be wiped out.

There was no way Carlie was going to let anyone wipe out the threat of one tiny little life. Timothy was a blond-haired angel, with nothing like Hector Mendino's heavy, brutal good looks. He probably looked like the American soldier who'd married Caterina. The American soldier who should arrive, sooner or later, to collect his son and wife, only to learn he was now a widower.

The fighting had been growing steadily closer to the mountain area surrounding the convent. At night Carlie would lie in bed and listen to the sound of gunfire in the distance. Timothy lay in the crib near her narrow cot, and the sound of his light, even breathing would calm her. Nothing, nothing would be allowed to hurt him.

She'd moved into Caterina's room in the infirmary, rather than drag all the baby paraphernalia back to her tiny cell. Caterina's clothes still hung in the closet, her jewelry sat in a small satin bag on a table. All except for her wedding ring. Billy Morrissey would want that, she knew, when she told him of Caterina's death. She'd slid it on her own hand, keeping it safe for him.

She was miserably hot and tired. Timothy hadn't slept well the night before, and consequently neither had she. The generator was out of fuel, there was no way to cool the place, and the current thick heat was worse than she could ever remember. The baby was napping peacefully now, his diaper changed, his tiny belly full, his miniature thumb tucked in his mouth. Without hesitation Carlie stripped off the heavy layers of clothing that comprised her old-fashioned habit, ruffled her fingers through her short-cropped hair and headed for the shower.

The water was blessedly cool as it sluiced over her body, and she stood beneath its fall, comfortable for the first time in days. In all these years she'd never grown accustomed to the heat. Sister Mary Agnes used to tease her, tell her she should go back to the States and join an order that advocated modern clothes and air-conditioning. And Carlie had managed to smile in return, secure in the knowledge that no one would ever make her go back.

She stepped from the shower, reluctant to leave its coolness, and pulled one of the threadbare towels around her body. Timothy would sleep for hours now, and Carlie couldn't afford to waste time daydreaming in the shower. There were diapers to fold and some sort of meal to forage. Beans and rice, her staple, would have to do, washed down with water. It had been all she'd had to eat for weeks now, and her bones were beginning to stick out. She glanced at herself in the mirror as she continued to towel her body dry.

It was just as well she'd chosen a religious life, she thought wryly. She was hardly the epitome of any man's dreams.

She was too short, barely topping five feet. Too skinny, with small, immature breasts, narrow, bony hips and small, delicate hands and feet. Her dark hair was hacked off as short as it could go, since it was usually tucked under a simple white wimple. She looked into the mirror and saw her parents' faces staring back. Her mother's blue eyes, her father's dark brown hair and high cheekbones. Her mother's stubborn, generous mouth and short nose. Her father's pale skin and freckles.

Her face was all she had left of them. They were long dead, their blood soaking into the jungle floor of San Pablo, as was the blood of so many others. She would be damned before she let them hurt Timothy, as well.

There was no noise beyond the closed door of the bathroom. Timothy still slept soundly. And yet Carlie paused, her hand on the doorknob, the oversize towel draped around her body, all her senses suddenly alert.

She heard it then. A sound so faint it was almost indiscernible. A faint, scraping sound, as someone moved about the bedroom.

She turned, looking around the bathroom, but she'd left her long black habit tossed across the bed. There was one window in the room, high up, but she could reach it if she stood on the toilet. She could climb through—she was small enough to fit—and she could be away from there before the intruder even realized she was gone. She could be gone, but she would have to leave Timothy behind.

There was no question in her mind. The towel was threadbare but the size of a small blanket. She wrapped it around her more securely, reached for the door and opened it, as silently as she could.

He was leaning over the crib. At first all she could see was his back, his long legs, dressed in camouflage and khaki, and she felt a sick knot of dread in the pit of her stomach. "Don't touch him," she said, wanting to sound dangerous, but the words came out in a breathless plea.

He turned slowly, and there was a gun in his hand. A very large, nasty-looking gun, pointed straight at her.

For a moment all she could see was the weapon. If he shot her, who would take care of Timothy? Panic clouded in around her, but she fought it, lifting her head to stare at his face.

That's where she got her second shock. This immense, dangerous-looking man pointing a gun at her was no member of Mendino's black-shirted brigade, and no ragtag revolutionary ready to kill for his beliefs. The man staring at her through eyes the color of amber was undoubtedly an American.

"Billy?" she managed to choke out, stepping toward him, out of the shadows, ignoring the threat of the gun.

It was no longer a threat. He tucked it in his belt, staring at her, an unreadable expression in his eyes. "Don't you know your own husband, Caterina?" he responded.

She blinked. "You're not Billy," she said. She'd seen an old photograph among Caterina's belongings, and this man looked nothing like Billy Morrissey. The man in front of her was much taller, whipcord lean, with long dark hair that would be tolerated by no military. It was tied behind his head with a leather thong, and his face was cool, distant and severe. He was no kin to the tiny cherub still sleeping soundly. Therefore he was a danger.

"I'm Reilly," he said, as if that should explain everything.

It explained nothing. "Where's Billy?" she asked, fighting to keep her concentration. She glanced over at the bed. Her habit lay there, in an anonymous pile of black-and-white cotton, but there was no way she could casually stroll over and grab it.

"He asked me to come for you and the kid. What is it?" He turned back to stare down at Timothy.

"A girl," she said automatically. A girl stood a marginally better chance at surviving the male-dominated warfare of San Pablo.

He kept his back to her. "A girl?" he said. "Billy would've liked that."

"What do you mean by that?"

He turned back. "Billy's dead, Caterina. I'm sorry to be the one to tell you that, but the sooner you accept it the sooner we can get the hell out of here."

"I'm not Caterina," she said numbly.

He had a narrow, dark face. Not particularly handsome, but arresting. It twisted now, in a kind of gentle contempt. "Lady, I'm not in the mood for playing games. Billy told me where I'd find you. You're here, the baby's here and everyone else is long gone. Your clothes are in the closet, your jewelry's on the dresser and that looks like Billy's ring on your finger or I miss my guess. So don't try to tell me you aren't Caterina Morrissey because I'm not going to believe it."

"All right," she said in a surprisingly steady voice. "I won't."

"I'll get you and the kid out of here and back to the States," he said. "I promised Billy and his parents I'd see to it."

"And how do you plan to do that, Mr....Reilly, did you say?"

"Just Reilly. I was in the service with Billy. I just had the sense to get out in time. But I've been trained, Mrs. Morrissey, by some of the best. I won't let anyone get to you."

"Don't call me that."

"Why? You rather be called Miss Mendino? That could bring trouble down on you real fast. Most people didn't like your father much, and they tend to hold grudges."

She stared at him for a moment. He must have realized she had just come from the shower and was wearing nothing but a towel, but he ignored it as unimportant. A good sign. He was a big man, with a sense of coiled strength about him. Not bulky, but very strong. He stared at her impassively, and that, too, was reassuring. He didn't care about her. He didn't care about the baby. He was simply doing his duty. A last favor for an old friend. And he didn't strike her as the kind of man who would fail in anything he set out to do.

"Call me Carlie," she said faintly.

"That's a hell of a nickname for Caterina," he said.

"It's what I'm used to."

He nodded. "How long will it take you to get ready?" His eyes drifted down over her body, impassive, incurious. Thank God, Carlie thought.

"A couple of days at the most. I have to pack enough for the baby, and I need to be in touch with Matteo—"

"Matteo's dead," Reilly said flatly. "He was killed a week ago by renegade soldiers. They were looking for you."

A wave of sickness and guilt washed over Carlie. "How do you know? How long have you been here?"

"Two days. I had to wait until it was safe enough to get in here. They're looking for you, you know. You and Mendino's grandchild. They're all around here."

"Who are? The rebels, or the soldiers?"

Reilly smiled then, a slow, cynical smile that still had an astonishing effect on his austere face. "Soldiers on the north side of the convent. Rebels on the south. Cliffs to the west. Jungles and swamp to the east. Choose your poison."

"It's up to me?"

"Hell, no. I just thought you might like being consulted. We're taking the jungle."

"There are pit vipers in the jungle."

"I'd rather face a pit viper than a political fanatic any day," Reilly said. "We'll leave at sunrise."

"I can't be ready—"

"We'll leave at sunrise, Caterina," he said. "Or I'll take the baby and go without you."

She stared at him. She had no doubt whatsoever he would do just that. No matter if he didn't know how to take care of a newborn, no matter if he had to strap him to his back amid grenades and rifles and machetes. He would do it, without a backward glance.

"I'll be ready," she said, allowing herself the sinful luxury of a glare.

There was no sign of triumph on his dark face. "I thought you would," he said. "Where do I find food in this place?"

"There isn't much. Beans and rice. And baby formula."

"It'll do," he said in a neutral voice. "I think I'll pass on the formula, though. Aren't you breast-feeding?" Those embarrassingly acute eyes dropped to the direction of her chest with all the interest of a farmer checking a breeding sow.

Carlie had already pulled the towel closely around her, and her arms were folded across her chest. "You wouldn't believe me if I told you I wasn't Caterina, would you?" She tried one more time. She wasn't used to lying, but fate seemed to have arranged this without consulting her.

"No, I wouldn't believe it. Why aren't you nursing the baby?"

"I'm too flat-chested."

She was hoping to embarrass him. Instead she felt a flush of color wash over her. She had been in the convent, surrounded only by women, since she was seventeen, and in that time she had never considered discussing her breasts with anyone, male or female.

His eyes dropped again, considering. "Size doesn't have anything to do with the ability to nurse."

Carlie blinked. In her capacity as local midwife she already knew that, but she'd doubted the overgrown ex-soldier would be as knowledgeable. However, her embarrassment had reached fever pitch by now. "I'm not going to discuss anatomy with you," she said stiffly.

"Good, because I'm more interested in food than your breasts right now," he said in a cool voice. "Where the hell's the kitchen?"

The mortification vanished abruptly, replaced by anger. "You'll find it if you look hard enough," she said. "In the meantime maybe you'd let me get dressed."

Again his gaze swept over her body, and she realized he had absurdly long lashes in such a dark, masculine face. "Suit yourself," he murmured. "I'll make enough for both of us. But I wouldn't bother with too much clothing if I were you. It's hotter 'n hell around here."

Carlie thought of the enveloping habit lying on the narrow bed. It would serve him right if she appeared in the kitchen fully garbed.

But she wasn't going to. It hadn't been her idea, but the choice had been taken out of her hands. Sister Maria Carlos had already left for Brazil with the twelve other Sisters of Benevolence. Caterina Rosaria Morrissey de Mendino would go with Reilly and take her child with her.

There was no way she was going to entrust the baby to a stranger. She would see him safely out of there, and then she would tell him the truth. And not a moment before.

Chapter Two

Reilly closed the door quietly behind him, shutting Caterina Morrissey and her towel-draped body away from him. She wasn't at all what he had expected. He'd known Billy for almost fifteen years, and during all that time he'd never seen him fall for anything other than a stacked, leggy blonde. He'd assumed Caterina would be cut from the same cloth—Billy had certainly never said anything to lead him to expect anything else.

She didn't look like the stepdaughter of a notorious Latin American dictator. She didn't look like the pampered socialite who'd abruptly married an American army officer, run back home to San Pablo and her life of privilege when the novelty had worn off and then tried to rejoin him once she'd found out she was pregnant. The woman in the bedroom didn't have the face of a woman used to getting her own way.

But then, who the hell was he to know what kind of face she had? He'd been far too distracted by her body, though he was pretty sure he'd managed to disguise that fact.

Like Billy, he'd never had a weakness for small, strong women. He preferred the large, decorative sort. The woman clutching a threadbare towel around her wet body didn't seem like the kind who was used to having things handed to her. Maybe motherhood gave a spoiled brat character.

Interesting thought, but it was none of his damn business. He was there for one reason, and one reason only. To take Billy's baby home to the States, where it belonged. If Billy's widow wanted to come along, then fine. The Morrisseys would see to her, and unless motherhood had had a miraculous effect on Caterina Mendino she would be more than happy to hand the child over to her wealthy in-laws so that she could go back to enjoying life.

She hadn't realized just how thin the cloth of that enveloping towel was. He was hot, he was thirsty, and she'd stood there, glaring at him, fiercely determined to defend her child, and the water had beaded on her smooth, pale skin. He'd wanted to cross that room and lick the water from her throat.

Even now the notion made him grin wryly. She was deceptively appealing. It was no wonder Billy had married her, the man who always swore it wouldn't be fair to limit his attentions to just one woman. The woman in the other room had a subtle grace to her that was well-nigh irresistible.

It was a good thing he'd never been a slave to his powerful libido. It would take them a good four days to get back to the plane, and that was if they were extremely lucky, the weather cooperated and she wasn't the hothouse orchid he'd assumed she'd be.

She didn't look like a hothouse orchid. For all her slender bones she looked tough and strong. They might even make it out to the plane in three days.

He hoped so. She was distracting as hell. He wasn't interested in spoiled rich girls, in new mothers, in heiresses or in the tangled politics of San Pablo. He just wanted to get the hell out, so that he could get back to his place in Colorado. And get on with his new life.

She was right—the kitchen wasn't hard to find. And the food supply was pretty damn pathetic. Red beans, rice, a hunk of hard cheese wrapped in a damp cloth and canisters of formula. He picked one up. It weighed a ton, and he cursed beneath his breath. Why the hell couldn't she have nursed her own baby? It would have made life a hell of a lot easier.

She probably didn't want to ruin her small, perfect breasts. The cotton terry of the huge towel had been thin, worn. He had seen the shape of her breasts quite clearly the moment she'd walked into the room, and he'd found himself envying the baby. Apparently there was no need. That baby wouldn't get to taste those breasts any more than he would.

Still, there was no harm in fantasy, as long as he remembered that was what it was. He could dream all he wanted about Caterina Morrissey's breasts. He just wasn't going to touch.

IF THERE WAS ONE THING Carlie was unused to, it was men. Tall, young men. Men with dark, arresting faces, bold eyes and a lethal, unconscious grace. Not to mention the gun he carried. It was no wonder she was unnerved.

She wasn't used to swearing. The words *hell* and *damn* held a more literal meaning for her during the past nine years—they weren't used for punctuation.

And she certainly wasn't used to the clothes Caterina had brought with her to the Convent of Our Lady of Repose.

She stuffed the habit under the bed, squashing her instinctive guilt as she did so. Caterina's clothes still lay in the drawers, and Carlie searched through them in growing dismay.

Most of them, of course, were maternity clothes. Caterina had been a wealthy young woman, spoiled, self-absorbed, who possessed only the finest in clothing. Unfortunately most of that clothing was provocative, flimsy and huge on Carlie's smaller frame.

There was no bra that came even close to fitting her, so she had no choice but to dispense with one entirely. The silk shirts were fuchsia and turquoise, dangerously bright colors, and the pants were all miles too long. Fortunately her wardrobe came equipped with a number of fine cotton knit camisoles, and she could take a pair of scissors to the jeans and make herself cutoffs. When she finished she couldn't bring herself to look down at her body.

It had been so long since she'd worn jeans. So long since her arms and throat and head had been bare. She felt naked, exposed, vulnerable.

And cool.

She walked barefoot across the stone floor to look down at Timothy. He was sleeping still, worn-out from the night before, and she pulled the thin cotton coverlet over his little body, brushing her hand against his wispy blond hair. He had no father or mother, no one to love him and care for him.

No one but her. Caterina, her once-pretty face flushed with the fever that had ravaged her body, had clung to her hand during the last hours. "Take care of my baby," she'd whispered.

And Carlie had promised. She wasn't about to go back on that deathbed vow. Timothy was hers now, and she wouldn't relinquish him until she was certain she was doing the best thing for him.

She left the door open so that she could hear him as she made her way down the empty corridor to the kitchen. She could smell the food, and her empty stomach churned in sudden longing, her hunger overriding her nervousness.

Reilly was sitting at the table, eating slowly, steadily, his gun in front of him, close at hand. There was another place set across from him, a plate full of food and a mug of steaming liquid. She paused in the doorway, feeling faint.

"Coffee?" she whispered. "I used up the last of it two weeks ago."

"I brought some with me."

She moved slowly across the room, forgetting her exposed legs, forgetting her bare arms, forgetting everything but the food waiting for her. "What is it?"

"What you had. Beans and rice and cheese."

"Then why does it smell so good?"

"I can cook."

She paused by the side of the table, staring at him curiously, her self-consciousness evaporating beneath his impassive gaze. He was barely aware that she was female, a fact that brought her nothing but relief. It was hard enough being around a man like this. It would be even worse if he was aware of her as a woman.

"Not very many men can cook," she murmured.

"You just haven't met the right men, lady."

Lady, she thought. In her entire life no one had called her lady. Certainly no one had spoken to her in that drawling, cynical tone.

"I suppose not," she said, taking the seat opposite him. The coffee was hot, black and strong. She took a deep, scalding sip and felt courage race through her bones.

He'd already finished his meal, and he leaned back in the straight-backed chair that used to be reserved for Reverend Mother Ignacia and watched her. She was too hungry to be self-conscious at first, but gradually the coffee and the good food began to take effect.

"You're a cool one, aren't you?" he drawled.

She jerked her head up. "Why do you say that?"

"Oh, I wouldn't have expected any less. Given your jet-set life-style."

Treacherous ground, Carlie thought, reaching for her coffee. "Just how much do you know about me?"

"Not much. I never was one to read gossip columns, and you're a minor celebrity. Hell, I don't think you even get fifteen minutes of fame."

"I'd prefer it that way."

"Really?" He sounded disbelieving. "Don't you have any questions to ask me?"

"About what?"

His smile was far from pleasant. "Why, about the death of your husband? Don't you care what happened to Billy? Or do you believe there's no use crying over spilt milk?"

A wash of color flooded her face. "I care. I just...that is...I—"

"He died in a car accident," Reilly said in his cool, emotionless voice. "He was in D.C. visiting his parents. As a matter of fact, he'd gone to tell them they were about to become grandparents, and to prepare for a daughter-in-law. Unfortunately he always drove like a bat out of hell, and this time the roads were too icy. He slammed into a concrete wall and that was it."

"Oh," she said.

"Oh," he echoed, his voice heavy with sarcasm. "I was lucky to be near enough to make it to the hospital before he died. He asked me to make sure his kid was safe. You know anything about deathbed promises?"

The memory of Caterina's dark, fevered eyes still burned a hole in Carlie's brain. "A bit," she said faintly.

"Then you'll know that I'm bringing the baby back. And if you behave yourself, do as I say, then you'll get to the States, as well. But if I have to choose between you and the kid, the kid wins."

"As it should be," she said.

A flash of surprise lightened his eyes for a moment. "I imagine you'll find life in Washington to your liking," he said. "There are lots of parties, shopping, that sort of thing."

"What makes you think I'd stay in Washington?"

"That's up to you. But that's where the baby stays. With his grandparents."

"You think his grandparents have precedent over his mother?"

"I think you'll probably be ready to get on with your life. You're young enough, used to parties and having a good time. Why would you want a baby holding you back?"

"If you don't know, Mr. Reilly, I'm not about to explain it to you," she said in a furious voice.

"You might be marginally safer from your father's enemies in Washington, as well," he added in a non-committal voice.

"I beg your pardon?"

"You know as well as I do that you're in danger, no matter where you go. People have long memories, and not very fond feelings for your stepfather."

"What makes you think Hector Mendino's enemies are interested in me? Wasn't killing him enough?"

"Not for a true fanatic. They'll be after you, and they'll be after your kid."

She stared at him, aghast. "And that's what you're taking me back to?"

"You think you're safer here?"

"No."

"As long as you're with me, no one will get to you."

For some odd reason she had no doubt of that, but she fought against such implicit, uncomfortable trust. "You're pretty sure of yourself, aren't you?"

"I know my job," he said, his voice noncommittal. "Once you're in the Capital District the professionals can take over. I'm not interested in playing hero anymore. I've done my time. This is just a last favor to an old friend. I'll see you and the kid safely to the States, and then I'm gone. You'll never have to see me again. Understood?"

"Understood," she said, wondering why the notion of never seeing this man again should both relieve and disturb her. She'd met him less than an hour ago, she knew next to nothing about him, and he made her nervous.

She jerked her head up at the soft cry echoing down the corridor, a sound so faint most people wouldn't have heard it. He turned at the same time, caught by the same distant sound. "The baby's awake," he said.

"I know," she said. "You have good hearing."

"It comes with being a soldier. So do you."

"It comes with being a mother." It was amazing how easily the lie tripped off her tongue. A sin, one of many, and all so very easy.

He nodded. "I'll find some place to bed down. We'll be out of here by first light."

"I'll need to pack some supplies . . ."

"I'll take care of it."

"But you don't know what the baby needs. . . ."

"Lady, I've got a total of twelve nieces and nephews, ranging from two months to twenty-three years, and I helped raise my brothers and sisters. I know about babies.''

She believed him. At that moment she was ready to believe he knew about everything. Except who and what she was.

She nodded, rising. "I trust you." The moment the words were out of her mouth she wanted to call them back.

She'd never thought she would trust a man, especially one who had been a soldier, again. But this time she had no choice. Not for her own sake. But for Timothy's.

He didn't seem surprised. He simply nodded, leaning back in his chair and looking at her, as the faint thread of sound grew louder as the baby decided he was tired of waiting. "Smart of you," he murmured.

It was no wonder women chose to live such peaceful lives, cloistered away from men, Carlie thought as she rushed back toward the baby's room. She'd forgotten, or perhaps never realized, how vastly irritating men could be.

To be sure, they had their uses. Reilly would have no trouble shooting that gun he carried, and he would see them safely out of San Pablo, she had no doubt. He could also cook, and he came equipped with coffee. Things could be worse.

He also came equipped with an attitude, and presumptions, and a condescending manner that made her want to use those very words, and worse, that he dropped so casually into his conversation. And the fact that he was huge and undeniably good-looking didn't help matters. Particularly since he was probably all too aware of how his size affected people.

No, she didn't like him. But she didn't have to like him to trust him. By the time she reached Timothy he was wailing with unrestrained fury, and she scooped him up, holding him against her breast and murmuring soft reassurances.

"You'll never grow up to be a pig, will you, sweetie?" she cooed.

And Timothy, settling down into a watery snuffle, socked her in the eye with his tiny fist.

REILLY DRAINED THE LAST of his coffee. He'd given up cigarettes more than ten years ago, and there wasn't a day that went by that he didn't miss them. But right now had to be the ultimate. He would have killed for a cigarette.

Fortunately he wasn't given that choice—a deserted convent in the middle of a jungle was not the best place to find cigarettes. He would simply have to do without.

At least it might distract him from the memory of Billy's widow. Caterina—the name didn't suit her one bit. Granted, she was only half Spanish, but she looked more Irish than anything else, with her pale skin and blue eyes. Carlie suited her. Though he was better off thinking of her simply as Mrs. Morrissey.

He pushed away from the table and began packing tins of formula in a backpack. He hoped that tiny little creature in the crib was tougher than she looked. The next few days would be rough on the adults, including a woman who'd given birth not that long ago.

It was just too damned bad he couldn't afford to wait a couple of weeks, till the baby got bigger, till Carlie got stronger. Though she certainly looked strong enough, despite the unexpected paleness of her arms and legs.

But the soldiers were moving down from the north. The rebels were moving up from the south. Reilly had learned to trust his instincts in these matters, and he knew the whole place was about to go up like a firecracker. He needed to get those two safely out of here before it happened.

Why the hell did Billy have to fall in love with the daughter of a political hot potato? It would be tough enough if this was just any woman, any baby. But Mendino's only grandchild made it impossible.

Reilly didn't pay much attention to the word *impossible*. Not when there were no other alternatives. He was going to get Carlie and her baby out of San Pablo, safely back to the States, and then he was going back to his mountaintop, alone.

But before he left, he might give in to temptation and see whether her wide, pale mouth tasted as innocent as it looked.

"What are you doing?"

"Hell!" He whirled, the gun already drawn, as her voice startled him out of his faintly erotic reflection. "Don't ever do that."

She stared at him, at the gun pointed directly at her, and her huge eyes were even wider as she shifted the baby against her shoulder. "Are you always this jumpy?"

He shoved the gun back in his belt. "Let's just say I've got good reason. We're in the middle of a war zone, and no one around here is particularly fond of your family. What's wrong with the kid?"

"He's hungry."

"He?"

"I mean she," Carlie corrected herself, shifting the squirming baby in her arms. "I keep forgetting."

"There's a fundamental difference between boys and girls, Carlie. Or haven't you been changing the baby's diapers?"

"You'd know if I hadn't," she snapped, heading for the row of freshly washed bottles. She grabbed one and tossed it to him. "Maybe you'd better get used to doing this. Two scoops of powder, then fill it with the filtered water and shake it."

She must have expected him to refuse. Hell, he could rise to that challenge, and any other she wanted to throw at him. He caught the plastic bottle deftly, mixing up the formula. "Sure would be easier if you were nursing," he murmured, handing it to her when he was finished.

The baby obviously thought so, too. She was rooting around at Carlie's breast, making loud sucking noises. She made do with the bottle, however, when her mother tucked it in her mouth.

"I would if I could," she snapped.

He leaned against the table. He liked making her mad, he decided. She had too much of an otherworldly calm that she kept trying to pull around her. He didn't believe in other worlds. He didn't believe much in serenity, given the circumstances.

He liked watching her feed the kid, too, even if it was with a bottle. She was a natural mother, and the look she had as she bent over the baby was a far cry from her uneasy glares in his direction.

Maybe she wouldn't leave the kid with Billy's parents. Maybe she'd learned there were other things more important than parties and fancy clothes.

But that was none of his business. He was a courier, delivering his package safely. He needed to remember that.

Before it was too late.

Chapter Three

Carlie was used to the silence. She'd been virtually alone in the old building for the past three weeks, with only the baby and the jungle noises outside to keep her company. For all that Reilly was a large man, he moved with just as much silence as the most discreet Sister of Benevolence.

But she knew he was there. Even if she couldn't hear him, she could feel his presence, permeating the very air she breathed. Man, the invader, in this house of women.

She lay on the narrow bed, sweltering in the humid night heat. There wasn't even the hint of a breeze to cool her, and the jungle birds kept up their ceaseless chattering, while Timothy slept on.

She would be leaving this place in the morning, the only home she had known for the past nine years. Sometimes it seemed like the only real home she'd ever had, but she knew that wasn't the truth. There'd been other places, other homes. The first ten years of her life had been spent in California, where her parents had ministered to migrant workers. The next seven had been in a variety of places, always in her parents' footsteps, waiting for them to remember her existence among all the needy who ruled their lives.

Reverend Mother Ignacia said they died in grace. It didn't seem like grace to Carlie, hidden down behind the trees outside the small mountain town in the north where they'd been living. They had died in blood and pain, in a hail of bullets as they tried to bring their own version of God's words to the villagers. And Carlie had watched, frozen in horror and denial, crouched down with her fist shoved in her mouth to still her screams.

It was the harried relief workers who'd found her, who'd taken her down to the jungle convent of Our Lady of Repose, where Mother Ignacia and the others had clucked over her and soothed her and brought her reluctantly back into the sheltered world they lived in. As the years passed, no one seemed to remember she was there, and Carlie had grown secure, even as the country grew more explosive.

But now her safe life had come to an end. She would be back among the living, among the soldiers and the violence. She would put her fate, and that of Timothy, in the hands of a soldier, someone who killed. She had no other choice.

She heard a scream in the distance, and she sat bolt upright for a moment, her heart pounding. Then she lay back, trying to still her breathing. It was simply a jungle cat, out stalking its prey. Nothing to worry about. Nothing that could hurt her. Besides, it was the two-legged beasts she needed to fear. She'd known that for years.

There were no clocks in the tiny convent—the nuns ran their lives on God's time, not man's. Carlie hadn't noticed the lack before, but right then, in the middle of a heat-soaked night, she would have given anything to know what time it was. Whether it was getting close to sunrise, or if it was still worth struggling with an elusive sleep.

Where was Reilly? Sleeping in Mother Ignacia's bed? Prowling the night corridors? He looked like a man who would snore, but the only sound through the empty corridors was the occasional scream of the jaguar. Maybe he didn't need to sleep at all.

She did, but that blessed reward seemed to be denied her. The longer she lay sweltering on the bed, the worse it got. Finally she rose, pushing the rough cotton sheet away from her, and pulled on Caterina's clothes. She didn't bother to light the oil lamp by her bed—she didn't want to run the risk of waking the baby. Tiptoeing to the door, she opened it into the inky darkness of the hallway.

Her foot connected with something solid, and before she could stop herself she went sprawling onto the hard tile floor, onto the hard-boned body of her protector.

The words he muttered beneath his breath as he caught her narrow shoulders were words she'd forgotten existed. She scrambled away from him, ending up against the far wall, and as her eyes grew accustomed to the darkness she realized he'd been sleeping in front of her doorway, his bedroll a mute testimony to the fact.

"Sorry," she whispered, still mindful of the sleeping baby. "I didn't know you'd be there."

"Where'd you think I'd be?" he countered irritably. "It's part of my job."

She stared at him. In the murky light she could barely see him, but she realized belatedly that she'd felt hot, bare skin beneath her when she went tumbling over him, and she wondered just how much he was wearing.

"You could have told me," she said in a deceptively reasonable tone of voice. "What time is it?"

"Quarter past four. We'll be leaving in a little more than an hour."

"Then I suppose I shouldn't bother trying to get any more sleep."

"I suppose you shouldn't," he said, and she felt more than saw him rise, heard the rustle of clothing. "I'm going to scout around the place, see if we've had any uninvited visitors. You stay put till I get back."

"But—"

"Let's get one thing clear," he said, overriding her objections. "There's only one person in charge of this little expedition, and that's me. You'll do what I tell you, no questions asked, or I'll leave you behind. Your life might depend on obeying me. The baby's certainly does."

"Yes, sir," she muttered, struggling to her feet.

A large, strong hand came down on one shoulder, and she found herself pushed back down, this time onto his sleeping bag. "Stay put," he growled. And then he vanished into the darkness.

She started to get up, then paused. It wasn't like her to be defiant. She'd learned the safety and comfort of unquestioning obedience—why was she choosing now to rebel?

She sat back down again, tucking her feet under her and leaning her head back against the stucco wall. There was no sound at all now, except for Timothy's regular breathing in the other room and the steady pulse of her own heartbeat. The sleeping bag beneath her offered very little padding between her body and the hard tile floor, and it still retained his body heat. She considered lying down on the cool tiles, but she couldn't bring herself to do it. The steady sound of the baby mixed with the sultry stillness of the night, and Carlie felt her eyes begin to drift shut as she waited for Reilly to return.

It wouldn't be an easy hike out of there—she knew it far too well. Even under the best of circumstances they were at the treacherous edge of the rain forest, and the roads were narrow, rutted and overgrown.

Having two warring armies on their trail wouldn't help matters. Reilly would push, and push hard, and right then Carlie felt too weary to even crawl back to her own bed.

She stretched out on the sleeping bag, just for a moment. It smelled like coffee, and gun oil, and warm male flesh. She closed her eyes, oddly lulled by the faint, seductive odors, and fell asleep before she could stop herself.

THE FIRST RAYS OF DAWN were just beginning to penetrate the old convent when Reilly returned to the hallway where he'd spent a restless night. For a moment he frowned, certain that Carlie had ignored him and taken off. And then he saw her, curled up on his old army-issue sleeping bag, one small, strong hand tucked under her willful chin.

He stood over her, staring, but she didn't move, deep in a dreamless sleep. She looked younger in sleep, innocent, with that pale, delicate skin, that soft, unkissed mouth.

Though why the hell he should think of her mouth as unkissed was beyond him. She'd done a hell of a lot more than kissing, and Billy hadn't been the sentimental sort to be enticed by amateur lovemaking. The jet-setting daughter of Hector Mendino would have had more than her share of lovers, no matter how innocent she looked.

This time he heard the faint, snuffling cry of the baby before she did. She slept on, in an exhausted daze, while he moved past her into the bedroom, conquering the urge to lean down and touch her.

The baby lay on its back, snorting and snuffling plaintively. The look it gave Reilly when he leaned over the crib was unpromising, but it made no more than a token squawk of protest when he scooped it up, grabbed a folded diaper and headed back out toward the kitchen, stepping carefully over Carlie's sleeping figure.

By the time Carlie roused herself and wandered into the kitchen the coffee was made, the backpacks were loaded and ready to go and the baby was fed and dozing peacefully against Reilly's shoulder. She paused in the doorway, her spiky black hair rumpled around her pale face, yawning.

"Why didn't you wake me?" she asked, heading for the coffeepot.

"You looked like you needed some sleep. An hour or two isn't going to make that much of a difference in when we leave, and I'm used to babies."

She froze, the coffee halfway to her mouth, then turned to stare at him. At the infant resting comfortably against his shoulder. "I need to change her..." she began hurriedly.

"I already did."

She blushed. Odd, he wouldn't have thought someone like Caterina Morrissey de Mendino would be capable of blushing, particularly over something as innocuous as a baby's sex. "You want to revise your story just a little bit?"

She lifted her gaze to his, and the defiance in her soft mouth was more expected. "This is a Latin country, Mr. Reilly. The rebels wouldn't consider Hector Mendino's granddaughter to be much of a threat. His grandson, however, is a different matter."

She obviously expected him to object. Instead he simply nodded. "Find yourself something to eat, and then we'll get out of here."

"Where are we going?"

"Through the swamp to begin with. On foot, at least for the first day. I left a jeep about twenty miles down the track—if no one found it we'll be able to reach it by dark."

"And if someone found it?"

"We'd better hope they didn't," he said blandly. "We'll take turns carrying the baby. The damned formula weighs a ton."

"Would you stop picking on me about the formula?" she shot back. "I didn't have any choice in the matter."

He let his eyes drop. She was wearing just what she had worn the night before—a sleeveless white cotton T-shirt and cutoffs. No bra; he'd noticed that right off. Her breasts were small and perfect. Well, not perfect, if they couldn't feed a baby, he amended. But close to it.

"You'll be carrying the formula as often as I will," he said evenly. "We'll take turns with the baby."

"No. I can manage him."

"I never would have pegged you for a protective mother," he drawled, shifting the sleeping infant.

She looked more surprised than offended. "What do you know about me? We just met."

"More than you imagine. I know Billy's taste in women, and they run to thoroughbreds with expensive habits. Before I came down here I asked a few questions, and I didn't like the answers. You're a spoiled young woman, you married Billy on a whim, left him on a whim, and if you hadn't happened to get knocked up you probably would never have planned to go back to him. For all Billy's parents know, this might not even be their grandson."

"What do Billy's parents have to do with anything?"

"I told you, that's where I'm taking you. That's definitely where the baby's going. They have the money, the connections, to see to his well-being. If you want to hang around that's fine. It'll be up to you."

"A child needs family. Grandparents," she said slowly, as if she were just considering the notion. "Are they good people, these Morrisseys? Will they love Timothy, take care of him, teach him right from wrong?"

It sounded as if she'd already made up her mind to abandon him. "Trying to assuage your conscience? They've got money. They'll hire the best people to take care of him if they think he's their grandchild."

"I see." She reached out for the baby, and he put him in her arms. "And if they don't believe he's their grandchild?"

"I don't know if belief has much to do with it. They'll arrange for the proper blood tests."

"They don't sound like very nice people," she said in a quiet voice, cuddling the sleeping baby against her.

"What's nice got to do with it? The world hasn't got much use for nice. When it comes right down to it, money talks."

She lifted her eyes and looked straight at him. Innocent eyes, clear blue and honest. Why would someone like Caterina Mendino have innocent eyes? "Do you really believe that?"

"I've been around long enough. So have you."

She looked down at the child in her arms. "Maybe," she said. "But he hasn't. I don't want him to have to live by those rules."

"He *is* Billy's son, isn't he?"

"Go to hell, Reilly," she replied. And it must have been his imagination that her words shocked her.

IT WAS CRAZY, but for some reason Carlie was even hotter in Caterina's skimpy clothing than she was in her usual garb. The light cotton of her habit had flowed against her skin, letting air circulate around her. The knit shirt clung to Carlie's body like a blanket, making her itch. The weight of Timothy's tiny body in the sling-type holder added to the smothering sensation, and the backpack full of baby paraphernalia and the minimum of clothing must have been thirty pounds at least.

Reilly hadn't said a word as he loaded her down, other than to look askance at the shorts. "That won't be much protection against pit vipers," he said pleasantly.

"Then you'd better make sure none of them get to me," she'd retorted without hesitation. "Otherwise you'll end up carrying everything."

"Good point." He was already loaded down with at least twice the amount she was carrying, though it didn't seem to bother him in the slightest. He was looking dark and dangerous in the light of dawn, with a stubble of beard, his long hair tied in a ponytail, his rough camouflage clothes rumpled as if he'd slept in them. But he hadn't slept in them, she remembered. She'd felt warm bare skin beneath her hands. "Let's do it."

"Do what?"

He paused, staring at her in baffled frustration. "Leave," he said impatiently. "Vamoose. Split. We're out of here. We're history. ¿*Comprende?*"

"*Sí,*" she said in a cool voice. "Spanish and English I understand. I'm just not too sure of the other stuff."

"Yeah, right," he muttered under his breath. "Keep quiet and stay close. And do exactly as I say."

"Yes, my lord and master," she retorted.

He didn't deign to answer her. He simply swung off down the narrow trail that led through the swampy undergrowth, with her following behind. She had more than enough time to think about her uncharacteristic behavior.

In nine years she'd never spoken in such a snippy tone. As far as she knew, she'd never felt the annoyance, the defiance that her reluctant rescuer brought out in her with nothing more than one of those long, calculating looks. She'd cursed, too, the word slipping from her as if it were entirely natural.

She was coming back to life, and she didn't like it. It was no wonder the Sisters of Benevolence had founded their convent deep in the heart of the jungle, away from the annoyances and distractions of civilization. The sooner Carlie found her way to the sister house in Brazil, the happier she would be.

Timothy would be fine. He had grandparents with money and privilege to look after him. She had no qualms about any blood tests—Caterina had made a halting, stumbling last confession to Carlie at the end, since there was no priest around, and while there had been any number of men before she met Billy Morrissey, she insisted that the baby was her husband's.

It would be hard to give the baby up; Carlie was honest enough to admit it. In the past few weeks it had felt as if Timothy were her own, and the bond had grown so strong she'd almost forgotten Caterina's sad, short life.

But he wasn't hers. Her life was with the Sisters of Benevolence, and sooner or later she would be able to convince Reverend Mother Ignacia of that fact. Timothy's life was back in the States, with his father's family.

She kept her eyes trained on the man ahead of her as he led the way deeper into the jungle. The sooner she got away from him the better. She knew perfectly well why she was suddenly full of frustration and temper, why blasphemies and more were simmering in her brain.

Convents existed to keep men and their distractions out. Women were much better off alone, away from the annoyances of the male sex. And that was what Carlie wanted to be—safe, alone, away from Reilly.

Unbidden, Mother Ignacia's words returned to her. Was she running away from something, rather than running to the sisters? She didn't want to be a coward, or someone with a weak vocation.

"This might be for the best," Reverend Mother had said. And Carlie could only trust her wisdom.

She would put up with Reilly's overbearing, disturbing presence. She would get safely away from San Pablo, relinquish Timothy and follow her calling, secure in the knowledge that it was a strong and true one.

She would weather these temptations and triumph.

Though why she should think of someone like Reilly as a temptation was a mystery. He was an attractive man, even with that long hair and unshaven face, but she was immune to such things. He was a strong man, when she needed strength, but he was a man of violence. She had seen enough violence to last her a lifetime.

The nightmares had stopped only in the past few years. Peace had finally come, and now it was being ripped away from her. She didn't want to remember. Didn't want to relive the day in the mountaintop village of Puente del Norte, when she could hear the screams, smell the thick, coppery smell of her parents' spilled blood washing down the streets.

She wanted nothing more than to run away and hide. Again, Reverend Mother's words rang in her head.

She would survive. She would accept Reilly's help, for her sake and the baby's. From now on she would be unfailingly polite, docile, obedient, as the sisters had taught her to be. Unquestioning, she would do exactly as Reilly ordered her, knowing that he would keep them both safe.

She would pull her serenity around her heavy-laden shoulders like a silken robe, and not a cross word would pass her lips. She managed a smile, thinking of the statue of the Madonna they'd left behind in the convent.

A branch thwapped her in the face as Reilly brushed ahead of her. "Watch what you're doing!" she snapped.

And somewhere, the Madonna laughed.

Chapter Four

The man wasn't human, Carlie decided three hours later. It was that simple. He was some sort of genetic mutation, produced by the American government to replace human soldiers in the field. No man could keep going, impervious to the heat, to the bugs, to the thick, sucking sludge at their feet, or to the weight of his pack, which probably had to be three times what she was carrying.

She was accustomed to the heat. Accustomed to pacing herself. Her pack was evenly balanced, and the baby slept snugly in his sling, content with the world and the no doubt thundering sound of Carlie's heartbeat beneath his tiny ear. Even so, the sweat was pouring down her face, her shoulders ached, her legs trembled and her feet were undoubtedly a royal mess.

There had been no shoes to fit her. The sandals that the sisters wore would provide little protection in the jungle, and she'd had to make do with Caterina's leather running shoes. Which would have been fine, if they hadn't been two and a half sizes larger than what Carlie would have normally worn.

She wouldn't have thought overlarge shoes would cause blisters. She was discovering she was wrong. The huge shoes were rubbing her skin raw, and she'd gone beyond pain into a kind of numb misery, plodding onward, only the sight of Reilly's tall, straight back giving her something to focus on and despise with a kind of blind fury.

"We have to stop." She had no idea how long they'd been walking, deeper and deeper into the swampy muck to the east of the convent. It was dark in there, and the trees so tall overhead that sunlight could barely penetrate. It was a true rain forest—the air thick and liquid, and the bush an overgrown tangle that Reilly hacked their way through.

He stopped, so abruptly that she barreled into him. He absorbed the force of her body, casually, and she registered once more how very strong he was. And how she found that strength alarming.

"Can't handle it, princess?"

His drawling tone shouldn't have annoyed her. After all, he was mocking the person he thought she was. He didn't know he was accusing Sister Mary Charles, a woman dedicated to poverty, chastity and obedience, of being a spoiled brat.

Nevertheless, the mockery rankled. "I can handle anything you can," she snapped back. "But we happen to have a baby with us. Timothy needs to be fed, he needs to be changed and he needs to be unstrapped from this contraption for a few minutes."

"I don't hear *him* complaining."

"That's because he's little enough that the rhythm of my footsteps is keeping him asleep. Sooner or later he's going to wake up and make it very clear how fretful he can be. He'll also probably leak through all the layers of clothing, and I don't have that many changes of clothes. I don't want to spend the day reeking of baby pee in this temperature.''

He turned to look down at her. ''You sound pretty fretful yourself,'' he observed with a faint smile. ''Okay, we'll rest. Half an hour, and no longer. We already got a much later start than I planned. You were the one who overslept.''

''You were the one who didn't wake me,'' she retorted instantly, and then stopped, appalled. What would Reverend Mother Ignacia say if she heard her? How many times would she have to remind herself of the vows she wanted to take? Hadn't she learned docility, obedience, the simple shouldering of responsibility whether it was deserved or not?

But Reilly didn't make her feel docile, or obedient, and she wasn't about to take responsibility for his decisions. She was out in the world, among men, thrust there by the vagaries of fate. For as long as she remained she might as well give in to temptation and let her emotions run free. For the next few days she'd give herself permission to feel anger. Fear. Tenderness. For the next few days she would give herself permission to live.

''True enough,'' he said, unmoved by what she considered to be a show of astonishing bad temper. He unshouldered his backpack and dumped it on the thick jungle floor, then reached for hers.

She backed away, suddenly nervous, but his hands clasped down over her shoulders, holding her there.

"Easy," he said, his voice roughly reassuring. "I was just trying to help."

She forced herself to be still, cradling the baby against her while he released the straps. The sudden relief as he lifted the pack from her shoulders was dizzying, and she swayed for a moment. Then he touched her again.

"Careful." This time his hands were on her bare arms. Rough hands, the skin callused. The hands of a man who worked hard.

She didn't stumble when he released her, but it took an enormous amount of effort not to. She sank down on the thick forest growth and released Timothy from the sling. He looked up at her out of sleepy blue eyes, opened his mouth in a yawn that swiftly turned into a mighty howl of fury.

"I know, precious, you're hungry, you're wet and you're hot," Carlie murmured. "Let me get these wet things off you and we'll get you something to eat." The soft clear sound of her voice stilled his rage for a moment, and he stared up at her as she deftly, efficiently stripped the tiny diaper from him, then fastened a new one. The convent had had a small supply of disposable diapers, and Carlie had crammed every last one of them in her backpack. She had no idea how long they'd last, but for the time being she had every intention of using them.

"How does that feel, little man?" she cooed, scooping him up. "Is it nice to have clean diapers and not be jiggled around all the time? Now just keep your temper for a few minutes while I make your bottle and..."

A bottle appeared in her line of vision—in Timothy's limited line of vision as well, and he immediately voiced his noisy demand. She took the bottle, settled back with Timothy sucking noisily, then allowed herself a glance at Reilly.

"Thanks for getting the bottle," she said.

"The sooner the kid gets fed the sooner we'll get back on the trail," he said, dismissing his actions.

Sweat was trickling down into Carlie's eyes, and she blinked it back as she looked down at the baby lying in her arms. He'd gotten bigger, stronger in the past few weeks. He was getting ready to smile, to hold his tiny, wobbly head up, to face the world. And she wouldn't be around to see those advances.

He made a squeaking sound of protest as her arms tightened around him involuntarily, and she immediately loosened her grip, feeling guilty. She couldn't give this child what he needed. And he couldn't give her what she needed. Even if it felt as if all she ever wanted lay wrapped up in his tiny body.

She glanced over at Reilly again. He'd thrown himself down on the mossy undergrowth, and he was busy searching through his pack. He had a kerchief tied around his forehead, his dark hair was pulled back and his khaki shirt was unbuttoned in deference to the wicked, soaking heat. She found herself staring at his chest, surreptitiously.

She hadn't had much experience in looking at men's chests, but she knew instinctively that this was a prime specimen.

His skin was smooth, muscled, dark with tan and sweat. He was lounging there, unconsciously grace-

ful, as he tipped back a canteen of water, and she
watched the rivulets escape the side of his mouth and
drip down his strong, tanned neck. She licked her lips.

She should have known he wouldn't miss that action. He rose, effortlessly, as if he hadn't been trudging heavy-laden miles through the jungle, and held out
the canteen for her.

She couldn't take it from him without letting go of
the bottle, and she knew very well just what the baby's reaction would be to that. She considered refus-
ing, but despite the liquid air her mouth and throat
were parched.

He didn't move, just waited. It was a challenge, she
knew that instinctively, though she wasn't quite sure
what was behind it. Control? Or something even more
unsettling?

He put the canteen against her mouth and she
drank, deeply, tasting the metallic flavor of the canteen and the warm, chemically purified water. Tasting his mouth, one step removed from hers.

He took the canteen away from her when she'd finished, without a word. And then he squatted next to
her, reached out and calmly fastened his spare bandanna around her forehead, brushing her hair back
from her face.

Her eyes met his, reluctantly, and for a moment she
sat there in the sultry heat as something strange and
disturbing flashed between them. Something inti-
mate, with his open shirt at eye level, the baby in her
arms, the quiet all around them.

She needed to break that moment, and quickly. She
didn't understand it, and it frightened her. Or per-

haps it was the fact that deep down she did understand it that was so terrifying. "Thanks," she said, tossing her head in an arrogant manner she'd seen Caterina perfect.

He blinked. For a moment his dark eyes shuttered, and then he rose, surging upward as if he were desperate to get away from her. "We need to keep moving," he said. "You want me to carry the baby for a while?"

"He's my child," she said instinctively. "I'll carry him."

Reilly shrugged. "Suit yourself. Let's go."

She started to protest, then glanced down to see that Timothy had fallen asleep in her arms, happily replete. She racked her brain for some way to delay, then gave up. The sooner they reached their destination, the sooner she could do something about her feet. Besides, hadn't she spent the past nine years of her life hearing stories of the blessed martyrs? Men and women who'd endured far worse than sore feet for the sake of their faith.

She wasn't doing this for her faith. But for the safety of a child, which was surely of equal value in God's eyes.

She waited until Reilly's back was turned before she rose, unsteadily. By the time he turned, instantly alert, she was composed, with Timothy settled back in the sling.

Reilly had her pack in one hand, holding the monstrously heavy thing as if it weighed no more than a feather. She braced herself for the added burden, forcing herself to give him a cool, unmoved look.

He was almost impossible to fool. He took in her defiant expression, her no doubt bedraggled appearance, and a faint smile skimmed across his mouth before vanishing once again.

"I'll carry your pack for a while," he said, shouldering it effortlessly.

"You don't need to baby me," she said instantly.

"I'm not. I'm trying to maximize our speed. We'll move faster if you aren't dragging your feet."

She could barely lift her feet, but by sheer force she kept her gaze on his face. "How much farther are we going?"

"Today? At least another ten miles. With this kind of brush that'll take us the rest of the day. Think you can handle it, princess?"

"Why don't you like me, Mr. Reilly?" she asked in a bewildered voice. "What have I ever done to you?"

"I don't dislike you, lady. I don't even have an opinion."

"Now that's a lie," she said flatly. "You've got plenty of opinions, and you formed them long before you showed up at the Convent of Our Lady of Repose."

"As I said, you've got a reputation."

"And you believe in reputations?"

He surveyed her for a moment. "Tell you what, lady. I'll forget about your reputation and judge you by your actions. Okay?"

"Judge me? What gives you any right to judge me?"

"It's human nature."

"That doesn't make it commendable. And my name's not lady. It's Carlie."

"Better than Mrs. Morrissey," he agreed, and there was no missing the faint barb in his voice. "Okay, Carlie. Let's get moving. I don't want to have to stop again."

"Tough," she said flatly, like the sound of the word. "Timothy will need to be changed and fed."

"And if we don't stop?"

"I'll let you carry him if he gets really soaking. And he's got an amazing set of lungs. Unless you think we're the only human beings in the jungle."

His mouth thinned in irritation, and she knew she had him. "We'll stop in two hours. No sooner."

Years ago, when she'd been brought down from that mountain village where her parents and all the villagers had been slaughtered, she'd found herself able to lock her mind away in a dark, safe place, so that nothing could touch her. She brought that place up again as she walked, mile after miserable mile, keeping pace with Reilly's fiendishly long legs. Timothy slept on, not even giving her the tiny respite another feeding would have afforded her, but she found she was grateful. If she stopped, and sat, she might never get up again.

It was growing steadily darker, some distant part of her brain told her, but she paid little heed. Until she was suddenly halted, and it took her a moment to realize that Reilly had turned and stopped her, his hands on her forearms.

She looked up at him, dazed, uncomprehending. "We're stopping for the night," he said harshly.

She blinked, then looked around her. There was no sign of a vehicle, no sign of civilization. Merely a sluggish stream winding its way through the undergrowth.

"Why?" she asked.

He'd already dumped both packs. His hands were gentle as they reached out and released the baby from the sling. Timothy was suddenly, furiously awake, but Carlie was beyond noticing. "Because you can't make it any farther."

From some place deep inside she managed to summon up a trace of indignation. "I can keep going...."

"Maybe. But you wouldn't be going anywhere tomorrow. Enough of the early-Christian-martyr bit, Carlie. Take your damned shoes off."

She would have thought she was too weary to react, but the reference stung. Could he read her mind as well? She was about to protest, but Reilly had already turned his back on her.

She walked straight into the shallow stream, shoes and all, then sat on the bank as pain made her dizzy. She could hear the baby's noisy protests, but she couldn't bring herself to move. Within a moment he'd stilled, and there was blessed silence, broken only by the quiet sound of the slow-moving water and the call of the jungle birds.

She lay back against the grass, groaning softly, staring up into the leafy canopy overhead. Every muscle in her body screamed in agony, and not even for Timothy's sake could she rouse herself. She was never going to move again. She was going to lie here in the jungle, her feet in the water, and die. Reilly was a responsible man who knew his way around babies. He could get Timothy out of there. For now she was just going to drift....

HE STARED AT HER. She had long legs for such a little thing, and sun had penetrated the rain forest just enough to give her a faint dusting of color. She lay beside the river in an exhausted stupor, probably asleep.

It was just as well. He found her distracting when she was awake. Hell, he found her distracting when she was asleep, as well, but at least she wouldn't be aware of it.

Timothy lay on his stomach on his discarded shirt, cooing happily enough, his diaper clean, his stomach full. They were going to need to get supplies before too long—their purified water wouldn't last forever, and Timothy seemed to be going through the stash of disposable diapers at an impressive rate. Reilly worked swiftly, efficiently, setting up a protective tarp, laying out their bedrolls. He didn't think Carlie was going to look with approval on the sleeping arrangements, but that was too damned bad. He had only one tarp, and the best way to keep the baby safe was to keep him surrounded by adults. Besides, Reilly was hardly going to jump her bones with a month-old infant as chaperon.

Besides which, she wouldn't be ready to have her bones jumped for another few weeks, even if she looked as if she was pretty well recovered from childbirth. She was off-limits, for every reason he could think of. Now why couldn't he remember that?

She wasn't what he'd expected. He hadn't had time to do his research before he took off for San Pablo. Things were in a crisis situation, as usual, and he couldn't afford to wait even an extra twenty-four hours so he could know what he was getting into. All he could go on was stuff he'd picked up, mainly by osmosis, and what he knew of Billy's taste in women.

None of it was to Carlie's credit. And he was too old and too experienced to be suckered by an innocent face and a vulnerable air. She was about as vulnerable as one of Mendino's black-shirted enforcers.

Still, she was pretty. Not drop-dead gorgeous, as Billy had assured him. Not stunning, not glamorous, not sophisticated. Pretty. He couldn't remember when he'd last used the word.

It made him think of cottages in England. It made him think of spring flowers, and baby lambs, and all those stupid things that made up camera commercials.

But she was brave. She'd stood up to him, when he'd been doing his best to terrorize her. He figured his best chance was to make her so scared she'd do everything he told her to, without complaining. He could be extremely intimidating when he set his mind to it. But Carlie didn't seem to be easily intimidated.

She was strong, uncomplaining. He knew she'd been in pain, but she hadn't said a word. And she was a good mother. The way she looked at her little baby, cooed to him, forgave a lot of sins. She'd do what needed to be done, he felt it in his bones. Maybe he didn't need to come down so hard on her.

He walked over to the stream. She was asleep, as he'd guessed, and her eyelashes lay against her cheeks. There was a faint flush of color in her face, but apart from that she was white and still. He looked down at her feet. And then he saw the blood.

He started to curse, rich, colorful invectives that could have turned the air blue, as he reached down under her armpits and hauled her out of the water. She hit at him, dazed and disoriented by the rude awakening, but he didn't give a damn. He simply dumped her farther up on the riverbank, still cursing, and then knelt by her sodden, blood-stained feet.

"Don't you have more sense than that?" he demanded when his first string of curses had run out. "Piranhas are the least of your worries in this climate. You lie there, trolling your bloody feet like some goddamn fishing lure while you take a little nap...." His voice was savage as he gently, carefully pried off her sodden running shoes.

There was no way he could keep from hurting her, especially once he got a good look at how bad they were. But she didn't say a word, simply clamped her teeth down on her full lower lip as he pulled the wet canvas and leather away from swollen feet.

"Whose shoes are these?" he demanded. "Don't you know better than to take off into the jungle without the proper footgear?"

"Piranhas are greatly overestimated," she said faintly. "They're not nearly as dangerous—"

"They're not nearly as dangerous as I'm feeling right now," he interrupted ruthlessly.

"For your information, I don't happen to have decent shoes with me," she said. "I wasn't expecting to go running through the jungle, and I didn't have a chance to go shopping before I left La Mensa."

"There hasn't been anything to buy in La Mensa for the last year and a half, and you know it." He sat back and looked at her feet. They were swollen, bloody, a complete mess. God only knew what kind of tropical diseases she'd picked up from the muddy water. He reached behind him for the backpack and the first-aid kit. "I'm going to have to hurt you."

He expected a smart crack. She didn't make one. She simply looked at him, out of those big innocent eyes that he couldn't believe in, and waited.

He was fast, deft and careful. He'd done more than his share of field triage, and Carlie's injuries, as nasty as they looked, weren't life threatening, once he got them properly taken care of.

When he was finished he sat back on his heels. "I don't know if you'll be able to walk tomorrow...."

"I can walk."

"Maybe we should wait a day."

"Is it safe?"

"No."

She looked at the baby, now sound asleep on the discarded shirt. Dusk had settled down around the jungle, and Reilly felt an odd chill run across his skin. "I can walk," she said again, and he had no doubt she would, if she had to do it barefoot on hot coals.

"All right," he said mildly enough, not interested in arguing with her. "Why don't you go lie down and I'll get you something to eat? Unless you need to use the woods?"

"Use the woods?"

"Go to the bathroom, lady. If you want I can carry you."

She blushed. A deep, embarrassed red. He stared in fascination. Why would she blush over something like that?

"I can manage," she said stiffly, starting to climb to her feet.

She didn't get far. She fell back with a muffled cry of pain, and he caught her. He didn't bother arguing with her—she was ridiculously small and light, and he simply scooped her up in his arms and carried her a little way into the brush, dumping her on her butt.

"Call me when you're done," he said.

"I don't need—"

"If you don't call me, I won't let you out of my sight again." His voice was implacable.

She glared at him, some of the dull apathy of pain fading. "You're a bully, aren't you?"

"Be glad of it, lady. It'll keep you and the kid alive."

Chapter Five

She didn't like being carried by Reilly. She didn't like being touched by him. His hands were big, strong, callused. His body was warm, sleek, muscled, and he hadn't worn a shirt. When he'd scooped her up and carried her through the woods he'd doubtless thought of her as nothing more than another burden, like the too-heavy pack.

But she couldn't dismiss the sensations so easily. The feel of that warm, smooth skin beneath hers was disturbing. Upsetting. It took her a full five minutes to get her senses back in order, to calm the emotions that roiled up inside her.

He was there to help her. The fact that he caused all sorts of strange, inexplicable reactions within her was simply the result of loneliness and stress. She needed to remind herself that while he was far from the friendliest soul in the universe, his motives were beyond noble and downright heroic. She needed to remember that, and not let her emotions and her unlikely irritation get in the way.

She didn't make the mistake of not calling him when she was finished. He wasn't a man who made empty threats, and she had little doubt he'd stand over her while she accomplished her calls of nature if she didn't do as he told her.

He picked her up again as if she weighed no more than the baby. He'd pulled on a dun-colored T-shirt, which made things marginally better, but it still took all of Carlie's concentration to ignore the bulge and play of his muscles when he lifted her.

The gathering dusk sent eerie shadows around the small clearing. It was then that she noticed the sleeping bags, side by side beneath the makeshift tent. The baby lay on his stomach, sound asleep in the middle of the conjoined beds.

"Are you sure we can't go any farther tonight?" she asked, suddenly nervous.

"You aren't in any shape." He dropped her down on one end of the bedroll. "Crawl in."

"What about snakes?" She glanced around, trying to appear cool. "Or jaguars?"

"Don't worry about it. I'll keep you safe from jungle beasts."

She peered up at him. He looked rather like a magnificent beast himself, looming over her in the darkness. "How?"

"I'll be keeping watch." He sat on the ground and began to crawl beneath the tarp. She watched him for a moment, disconcerted.

"How are you going to do that if you sleep?"

"I'm not going to sleep."

"Then why are you lying down?"

"Because I'm tired," he said, stretching out. And that was when she noticed the big, heavy handgun he'd placed by his head.

"But if you're tired and you lie down, then won't you..."

"Lady," he said wearily, "I was in the military for more than fifteen years. I was trained for combat, and I've spent the better part of those years in places where I couldn't afford to let up for a minute. I've never fallen asleep during guard duty and I'm not about to make a habit of it. Now get in the damned bed."

All her noble resolve vanished in a wave of pure annoyance. "What if I don't want to sleep with you?"

He closed his eyes in weary exasperation. "If I wanted to get in your pants you'd know it. For now all I want is for you to be quiet and climb in your sleeping bag. Preferably without waking the baby."

She didn't have any choice in the matter, and she knew it. Timothy lay sleeping peacefully enough, and Reilly looked as if he found her about as interesting as a day-old slug. She slid down, stretching full length on the sleeping bag and closed her eyes determinedly.

She listened to the silence, trying to will herself to sleep. Until she heard the unmistakable sound of chewing.

Her eyes flew open. He was stretched out beside her, and he was eating something brown and nasty looking that nevertheless had her stomach churning in hunger.

"Are you planning on sharing that?"

He glanced over at her, and there was just a hint of amusement in his dark eyes. "I didn't think you were interested in food."

"I'm interested. What is it?"

"Dried beef jerky. We also have an assortment of dried prunes, dried apples and trail mix."

"Yummy," she said wryly. "Where is it?"

"Ask me nicely."

She reached out and snatched the piece of meat from his hand, scuttling out of his way before he could grab it back. Between them the baby slept on, secure between the two battling adults.

"I don't suppose you have any coffee?" she asked after a moment.

"All out. If we manage to make it to the jeep tomorrow we should be able to get supplies. Maybe even a bed for the night, though I'm not certain I want to risk it. Are you going to be able to walk?"

She wiggled her feet carefully. They hurt, but the salve Reilly had rubbed into them seemed to have done wonders. "I think so."

The night was growing darker around them, so that she could barely see him in the small confines of the makeshift tent. She heard him move, and a small pack of trail mix landed in front of her. "Where's your canteen?" he asked.

"I don't know. Besides, I'm not particularly thirsty."

"Damn it, woman, you can't go losing your canteen," he snapped. "And I don't care whether you're thirsty or not. In this climate you can get dehydrated real fast, and then I'd have two helpless creatures on my hands.''

"Reilly, my name isn't woman, it isn't lady, and it isn't princess. It's Carlie.''

"It's Caterina Morrissey," he reminded her. "And I don't particularly like that fact.''

"Why not?''

"Maybe it reminds me that a buddy is dead, and that before he died he got suckered by a spoiled jet-setter.'' He shoved his canteen at her.

She didn't make the mistake of not taking a long drink. She might not be able to see him clearly in the dark, but she wouldn't put excellent night vision past his extraordinary list of capabilities. What in the world had Caterina ever done? Her deathbed confession, a talk shared between two unlikely friends and far from a religious ritual, hadn't been specific. It had been the weary cry of a wasted life that had once been full of promise, and it had broken Carlie's heart.

"Maybe you should think instead that he left a son behind," she said in a relatively calm voice. "And the spoiled jet-setter who suckered him is responsible for something of him continuing in this world.''

"Maybe," he said, not sounding particularly convinced. "Go to sleep. I'm willing to bet the baby won't be sleeping through the night, and I sure as hell don't want to be feeding him and changing his diapers.''

"You have already," she said sleepily, stretching out on the sleeping bag. "I'm surprised I haven't heard you complain before. You're very good with babies.''

"I'm good at what I need to do. And I don't complain if things can't be helped. You might work on that, princess."

"Have you heard me complain yet?"

"No."

"You won't."

There was silence for a long moment. She waited, half expecting him to come up with another barbed comment. But her eyes drifted closed, and she told herself he wasn't about to give an inch.

And neither was she.

SHE WOKE DURING THE NIGHT. She lay still in the darkness, listening to the light, peaceful sound of the baby sleeping beside her. Listening to the steady, even breathing of the man who lay just on the other side.

She could feel his body heat in those close quarters. She could smell the scent of coffee and gun oil and sweat that clung to both of them. She lay there and listened, wondering if he slept. Wondering if they'd be safe from marauding beasts, wondering if a bushmaster was going to slither into her sleeping bag and...

"Go back to sleep, Carlie." His voice was nothing more than a deep whisper of sound. "I'm not going to let anything happen to either of you."

She should have resented him. She had learned to put her trust in nothing but God, and a hostile man in camouflage with a gun wasn't the first likely person she'd feel like cozying up with.

But fate, or God, wasn't taking her feelings into consideration. And despite her fears, her doubts, her misgivings, she knew perfectly well that the man lying beside her would be true to his word. Nothing would get past him. Nothing would harm the baby. Nothing would harm her.

Except, perhaps, for this unwanted excursion into the real world, complete with men and guns and life.

But she would survive. And for the time being she was perfectly safe, with Reilly watching over them. Closing her eyes, she sank back into a deep, dreamless sleep.

THEY WERE ON THE TRAIL by a little past dawn the next morning. Reilly wasn't in the mood to be impressed, but he had always considered himself a fair man, and Billy's little princess had done herself proud. She could walk, gingerly, but with the bandages she'd wrapped around her feet those oversize running shoes fit her. She fed and changed the baby, ate trail mix without a murmur and even managed to look gorgeous when she struggled to her feet and began to hitch the kid into that sling-type thing she wore.

"Think you can make it another seven miles?" he asked, shouldering both their packs.

He saw her blue eyes blink at the number seven, but apart from that she showed no distress. "Yes."

"Good." He started through the forest, leaving her to follow along behind him.

He moderated his pace, just enough to make it easier on her, not so much that it would endanger them. Not so much that she would notice. Carlie Morrissey was turning out to be a far cry from the woman he'd expected, but she did have her share of pride. She wouldn't like knowing he was going easy on her. Hell, he didn't like knowing it, either.

They walked in silence for the better part of an hour, listening as the jungle awakened around them. The screech of the macaws, the random scream of the jaguar floated on the thick, liquid air, and Reilly felt the sweat pool at the base of his spine.

Damn, he hated the jungle. Hated this smothering heat, where a man couldn't breathe without filling his lungs full of ooze. He knew that accounted for part of his bad attitude toward Carlie. He wanted to be back on his mountaintop in Colorado, not hacking his way through the undergrowth with a woman and a baby behind him. He'd had enough of jungles in his life. Enough of heat. He wasn't sure which he hated more—the steamy tropical forests of Latin America, or the dry, searing heat of the Middle Eastern deserts. He'd left the army because he was fed up with heat, fed up with stupid little wars and innocent people getting in the way. So where did he end up? Smack-dab in a stupid little war, in the heat, trying to save a couple of innocent people.

He owed Billy. He owed him his life, he owed him anything Billy would ask. It was too late for that. But bringing his kid and his playgirl wife back to the States would even out a lot of old debts, even if he paid them beyond the grave. He could put up with a little heat and discomfort for that, couldn't he?

What he was having a hard time putting up with was Caterina Morrissey. He was fine when he thought of her as Caterina, when he didn't look so closely at her, when he kept himself wound so tightly that nothing could sneak through.

But when he looked at her, really looked, at the absurdly innocent eyes and vulnerable mouth, at the small, coltish body and the instinctive, natural grace, at the love she poured on that red-faced little baby, he found himself thinking other, dangerous thoughts. Like how Billy must have misjudged her. Like what a lucky man he'd been. Like what would she taste like if he kissed her. Like how long did it take for a small woman like her to recover from the physical trauma of childbirth.

He hadn't thought much about having kids of his own. He'd been too busy, there'd been no special woman and his horde of nieces and nephews had provided him with more than enough kids to last him.

But if he did get married, did find a woman to share his mountaintop, he'd want her to be just a little like Carlie. Not Caterina, the spoiled bitch, who'd married Billy, left him when she grew bored, and only came back when she found out she was unexpectedly pregnant and her cozy little life in San Pablo was collapsing.

No, he'd want her to be like Carlie, who snapped at him, trudged along behind him uncomplaining, and who loved her baby.

The terrain that comprised most of San Pablo was like no other place in the world. Half rain forest, half jungle, it was home to pit vipers and jaguars and hundreds of varieties of flesh-eating fish and birds that had never been cataloged or identified by the scientists who'd braved the revolutions and the natural dangers of the land to document the wildlife. And among all those deadly species, none were quite so threatening as the fanatical armies of San Pablo, the black-shirted goon squads of Hector Mendino and Endor Morales, his notorious general, and the ragtag rebels who wouldn't think twice about slaughtering an innocent baby who might someday pose a threat.

He didn't like it here, Reilly thought sourly, trudging onward. Hell, he didn't like it anywhere nowadays, except for Colorado. He'd spent too much time in San Pablo in the past, but he'd forgotten how bad the climate could really be. He wanted out of here, and he wanted out, fast.

He glanced back at Carlie. Her face was pale beneath the hot pink flags of sunburn against her cheeks, and her eyes were dull with exhaustion. She walked slowly, without limping, the baby cradled against her, and he wondered how much longer she was going to manage to keep going. If worse came to worst he could always carry her. She was a tiny thing, hardly big enough to have given birth to even a baby as small as Timothy. He couldn't imagine her lying beneath someone like Billy Morrissey, who'd been built like a linebacker.

He quickly shut off that line of thought. It was none of his damned business whether she was beneath or on top. The sex life of Caterina Morrissey was none of his business at all.

He halted abruptly, then turned, putting a hand on her shoulder to stop her. She looked up at him, her clear blue eyes dull and shadowed by exhaustion, her soft mouth grim. "We just stopped an hour ago,

Reilly," she said in that calm voice of hers. "You don't need to pamper me—I don't need another rest yet."

She needed a hell of a lot more than a rest, but he didn't bother pointing that out to her. "We aren't resting," he said. "We're here." He jerked his head toward the underbrush.

She peered around him. "Where? I don't see anything."

"I do. The jeep's still in there. Just give me a couple of minutes to check for sabotage and then we can start out of here. With luck we might make Dos Libros by nightfall. There's a cantina there, run by an old scoundrel named Dutchy. We could probably commandeer a bed for the night."

"One bed?"

His mouth curved in a wry smile. "This time I'll do the sleeping and you can keep watch."

She had the most expressive blue eyes. He could see every thought, every emotion as it flitted through. She was looking up at him, judging him, measuring him. "You look tired," she said flatly. "You had me thinking you were invulnerable."

"I get tired," he said. "I get hungry, I get thirsty, I get horny. I just don't do anything about it if it's not convenient."

She still didn't respond as he expected her to. "You didn't say whether you ever got lonely."

He thought for a moment, of the remote mountain cabin, half a continent away, with only the animals and his work for company. "No," he said flatly. Lying.

She didn't call him on it, as he'd expected her to. She simply nodded, sinking onto the thick grass and holding the sleeping baby against her. He handed her his canteen, and she took it without argument.

By the time he'd managed to clear the camouflaging brush away from the jeep, check over the entire thing and load up the packs, Carlie looked as if she were half-asleep. She barely made a sound when he loaded her into the front seat, not even protesting when Reilly took the sleeping baby away from her and strapped him in the infant seat he'd stashed with the gear. He almost teased her, but she sat in the cracked leather seat, and if the old army vehicle hadn't come equipped with webbed seat belts to hold her in place he expected she might very well have slipped right onto the floor.

She was asleep before he put the jeep in gear, and even the bouncing, rolling ride over the rutted path didn't wake her. He had less than a quarter of a tank of gas—enough to get them to the tiny village of Dos Libros and not much farther. He just had to hope that the tiny outpost there had a reasonable supply of fuel. Otherwise they'd be walking again, and he wasn't sure how his frail little jungle flower would hold up.

Except that she wasn't frail. She was little, but she was surprisingly strong, and he'd put her through a workout that would make an aerobics instructor collapse. And she wasn't his.

He needed to keep that firmly in mind. She was dependent on him right now, and she didn't like it. She also looked up at him with a kind of innocent wondering in her eyes that made him damnably uncomfortable. Though why someone with a reputation like Caterina Morrissey would be possessed of either wonder or innocence was beyond him.

He had to be careful. Billy's wife was the kind of woman who was used to having a man take care of her. Since he was the only one around, it would be only natural that she would turn to him. And he didn't want that.

He wasn't quite sure why. He had a healthy interest in sex, when it didn't interfere with other, more important matters, and he would be a fool to deny that he found Carlie... irresistible. There was no real reason he shouldn't have sex with her if she was willing and eager.

But he didn't want to. For the first time in his life he wanted the same woman Billy Morrissey had wanted. For the first time in his life he could feel the slow, strangling tendrils of longing for something more than the fast, hot release of sex. When he looked at the pale face of the woman sleeping beside him, he didn't see a manipulative socialite or a cheating wife. He didn't see a mother who would doubtless abandon her child the first chance she got, or a woman with a score of rich and powerful lovers.

When he looked at her he saw hope. And a dream. And it scared the bloody hell out of him.

Chapter Six

Carlie's eyes flew open in sudden, mind-shearing panic. She was alone, in the parked jeep, in the middle of a narrow jungle track. It was already growing dark, and the night insects were darting around her head. There was no sign of Reilly. No sign of the baby.

She tried to leap out of the car seat, but the seat belt held her back. She fumbled with it, taking forever to release the old clasp, telling herself not to panic. He wouldn't have abandoned her. Wouldn't have stolen the baby and left her alone in the heart of the jungle.

But then again, why wouldn't he? He'd proved he was more than capable of taking care of Timothy—he didn't need her around to feed or change him. She was just an inconvenience, something Billy Morrissey's family would have to deal with. Everyone would be a lot happier to know that Caterina Morrissey was really dead.

Maybe she should have insisted on telling Reilly the truth. She'd tried, but he hadn't believed her. What would he have done, once he'd known? Would he have taken the baby and left her behind? She'd promised Caterina she'd take care of her son, and she hadn't wanted to give him up. Perhaps this was God's punishment for her lies and her selfishness. Timothy would be better off with his grandparents, but she hadn't wanted to let him go.

Had Reilly been planning this all along? Why had he bothered taking her this far, only to abandon her to what was probably certain death in the night-shrouded jungle? Why hadn't she remembered what men with guns and uniforms were capable of?

She sat back in the car seat, pulling her legs up under her. The air had grown cool on her bare arms, and she shivered. If she were anyone else she would have had the luxury of tears. But it had been nine years since she'd cried, and she wasn't about to start now.

"Did you think I'd abandoned you?" The voice came from close behind her, drawing, laconic.

She whirled around in the seat, to see Reilly standing on the edge of the clearing, watching her out of wary eyes.

Relief and something more washed over her. She didn't even think, she simply moved, bolting out of the seat and racing across the clearing. She flung herself against him, babbling in relief and exhaustion.

"I thought you weren't coming back," she said against the soft cotton of his T-shirt. "I thought you'd left me her to die...."

His hands had come up to catch her arms, holding her, and she was vaguely aware of his strength. His warmth. His surprising tenderness. He didn't push her away. He simply held her there as she ranted, cradling her against his body, and she breathed in the warmth

and the scent of him, and the words ran down as she
let out a long, shuddering sigh.

"That's better," he murmured. He'd moved his
hand up to the nape of her neck, beneath her short-
cropped hair, and he was kneading the tension away
with his long fingertips. "I've found us a place for the
night. You were dead to the world when we got here,
so I decided to let you sleep."

She looked up at him, as the slow, sensual kneading erased the tension in her body. "I was frightened."

"You had reason to be."

His face was very close to hers. It came to her, belatedly, that she was standing in a man's arms, pressed
against his body. She stepped back, suddenly nervous, and he released her.

"Where's the baby?"

"Dos Libros is just over the rise. The women are
looking after him. I realize you probably aren't too
happy about the fact that I turned your son over to
strangers, but the women of the Shumi tribe are excellent mothers and nurturers, and I figured he would
be much safer."

"It's all right," Carlie said. "I trust your judg-
ment."

She'd managed to startle him. And then his mouth
curved in a faint smile. "That's good. Because I decided we'd better share a bedroom."

"I..."

"Keep your mouth shut and your head down," he
added, heading off the way he'd come, obviously assuming she'd follow. "I don't think the Shumi have

had much traffic with the outside world, but Dutchy has some dangerous friends, and he might very well recognize you. I don't want to raise any suspicions if I can help it."

"What did you tell the Shumi?"

"That you're my woman. That the baby is ours, and that I'm a very jealous man. The Shumi will leave us alone. I'm not so sure about Dutchy. He'd sell his own grandmother for a handful of pesos, and the reward on you and the kid is a lot higher than that."

She strained to match his steady pace through the underbrush. "Reward?" she echoed, not certain if she had heard right.

"Enough to keep me in style for the next decade," he said lightly.

"Are you trying to frighten me, Reilly?" she demanded, panting slightly as she struggled to keep up with him. "If you are, I think I ought to mention that there's no need to try quite so hard. I'm officially terrified."

He glanced over his shoulder, his eyes glittering in the darkness. "I'd say you're about as frightened as the Terminator," he drawled.

"What's the Terminator?"

"Give me a break, Carlie. You know what I'm talking about."

She didn't, but she obviously should have. If she'd lived anywhere near civilization for the past ten years she would have been conversant with the entity. "You think I don't get scared?" she demanded.

He stopped and looked at her. "Well, I don't know. I've already admitted I get tired and hungry and scared and horny. You have all those human weaknesses?"

"Most of them," she said carefully.

He laughed, and it wasn't an unpleasant sound. "We'll get you some food and some rest tonight," he said. "We'll have to see about the other stuff. In the meantime, you stick to me like glue. There've been bands of Mendino's ex-soldiers roaming the area, and Morales himself has been seen not too far from here. Not to mention the rebels, who are just as bloodthirsty as your stepfather's goons. I didn't bring you this far just to lose you."

"I have no intention of letting you out of my sight if I can help it."

"Why, princess," he said with a slash of a smile. "I didn't know you cared."

She'd seen tiny villages like Dos Libros, though not in the nine years she'd been cloistered with the sisters. Her parents had died in a village very much like this one, and the memory sent a shudder of remembered pain through her, one that she was able to hide from Reilly. She'd seen places like Dutchy's—a combination store, post office, bar and hotel, but most of all a hovel. There was no sign of the Shumi women, or Timothy for that matter, and she quickly stilled her flash of possessive panic, resisting her need to go after him.

"Get behind me," Reilly muttered under his breath. She quickly did as she was told, and he put his arm around her, pushing her face against his shoulder. She couldn't see anything, could only trust in him to steer her safely toward the door.

"This your wife, Reilly?" The voice was jovial, Germanic and not to be trusted for a moment. Even Carlie could tell that much.

"Close enough," Reilly drawled. "You got a bed and a shower for us, Dutchy?"

"Is the pope Catholic?" Dutchy responded. "I've also got a hot meal and the best whiskey in all of San Pablo. I make it myself."

"We'll take a bottle," Reilly said, pulling her toward the stairs. She could see her feet out of the corner of her eye, feel the other people watching her. Dutchy, and others, as well. "You can send it up to our room."

"Now, Reilly. You know how cut off we get around here. Starved for information, we are, aren't we, boys? You can't just hole up in your room with that pretty little thing. We want to know where you've been. What you've seen. These boys have to report back to their commander, and they need to hear about any trouble you may have run into. These are dangerous times, my boy, and we need to be prepared."

She didn't need to see Reilly's mocking smile to know his expression. "Information doesn't come free, Dutchy. And I'm more interested in having my woman in a bed for a change than gossiping. They'll have to go out and find their own information, instead of sitting around in a bar."

It was just as well her face was pressed against his body. The color flooded her pale skin, and her faint sound of protest was uncontrollable.

"You sure she wants that?" Another voice spoke, this time in Spanish. Slow, and menacing. "The lady seems uncertain. My men and I would be glad to provide her with an alternative."

They'd reached the foot of the stairs. She could feel the tension coiling through Reilly's body, the utter, deadly calm. He put his hand under her chin, drawing her face into the dim light of the building. The watching men were at a distance, the room was thick with smoke and the greasy light of oil lamps, and there was no way they could get a clear look at her. No way they could recognize the daughter of Hector Mendino in the face of a nun. "What do you say, woman? Are you interested in leaving my protection?"

She shook her head, staring at him in mute pleading. He turned, shielding her behind his strong back. "You see, gentlemen. The lady is not uncertain, merely tired and impatient."

"If she grows tired of you, hombre," the man said with a coarse laugh, "I'll be more than happy to step in. I have..." She didn't understand the rest of the sentence. She could guess what he was referring to, but she didn't want to. Color stained her cheeks once more as Reilly guided her up the rickety old staircase.

Dutchy was waiting for them, peering at her in the dim light. "Second door on the right, bathroom down the hall." He spat for emphasis. "You're our only guests right now, so it's a private bath. Fifty American dollars a night."

"You're the soul of generosity," Reilly said.

"A man must support himself the best he can. Just be glad the soldiers downstairs are moving on tonight."

"Why should it matter one way or the other?" Reilly said carefully.

Dutchy smiled, revealing chipped, stained teeth. "You tell me, amigo."

Carlie waited until they were in the tiny room. Waited until Reilly closed the door behind them and Dutchy's footsteps echoed down the hall. And then she looked around her.

It was far from reassuring. There was one bed in the room, a small, sagging iron one, with a faded chenille cover, two limp pillows and an oil lamp beside it. There was nothing else in the room.

"Where will the baby sleep?" she asked carefully, avoiding the more disturbing question.

"He'll stay with the Shumi. I figure he'll be safer there. Right now he's with the chief's wives, being treated like royalty."

"I wonder how they'd feel if they knew he was the grandson of the man who was responsible for the genocide of three-quarters of their population," Carlie said bitterly.

"It would make no difference. The Shumi revere children, even those of their enemies." He tilted his head, looking at her. "You don't sound too fond of old Hector yourself."

"He was a monster."

"That's right, he was your stepfather, wasn't he? Still, it was his money that provided you with your comfortable life-style. His death that took it away from you. I would have thought you'd be more grateful."

"His money was drained from the blood of the people."

"Are you certain you're not a revolutionary?" he asked in a lazy voice. "It's a little late to change sides—the rebels aren't going to welcome you and your son with open arms."

"They're just as bad. They're willing to kill anyone who gets in their way, all for the sake of their noble cause," she said bitterly. "And it's the children, the innocents, who get caught in the middle."

"Lord, what a bleeding heart," he said mockingly. "You ought to be a missionary."

It took her unawares, the sharp stab of pain. Suddenly she was seventeen years old again, on a hot afternoon in a mountain village, and her parents were being gunned down, they were screaming, she was screaming, there was blood....

"Stop it!" His voice was rough, hurried, as he yanked her against him. The room was hot, he was hot, and yet she shivered, unbearably cold and alone.

His hands were hard and painful on her arms, forcing her out of the miasma of horror. Back into reality, the here and now, which wasn't much better. "Stop what?" she managed to say faintly.

"You looked as if you were about to faint. Or scream. I'm not sure which would be worse." He didn't release her, though his grip had loosened slightly so that she felt the warmth, the strength, the imprint of each long finger as it wrapped around her arms. "Then again, I don't suppose either would be much of a problem. If you fainted I could simply dump you on the bed and not have to worry."

"And if I screamed?"

His smile was slow and dangerous. "There's a logical explanation for that, as well."

"What?" She was genuinely perplexed.

His smile faded, the stormy color of his eyes growing darker still as he watched her. "Lady," he said bluntly, "your love affairs have been the scandal of three continents. Don't tell me in all that time that no one ever made you scream when you made love."

She blinked. Her practical knowledge of sex was nonexistent, her theoretical knowledge so vague and so outdated that it was almost useless. She had only the faintest notion of what he was talking about, but she certainly wasn't going to ask him to explain. She tried to pull away, but he wasn't about to let her go.

"If they haven't," he continued, his voice low, disturbing, "then maybe I'll have to expand your horizons."

She held very still. He was going to kiss her. She knew it. She wasn't quite sure why—he hadn't shown much fondness for her up to now. But then, fondness didn't seem to have much to do with desire. She'd gathered that much over the years, from scraps of conversations she'd heard. It had never made much sense to her.

He gave her plenty of time to escape, to turn her head. But she couldn't. She felt mesmerized, curious, as his head dipped down, blocking out the light, and his mouth touched hers.

It was pleasant, she thought with surprise. The roughness of his beard, the firm contours of his mouth, the warmth of his body so close to hers were all quite...nice.

He lifted his head, and she took a startled breath. "That's very pleasant," she said ingenuously. "I think I—"

He didn't let her finish the sentence. His mouth came down over hers again, but this time it was open, against hers, and he was putting his tongue in her mouth. She tried to jerk away, but he'd threaded one large, strong hand through her hair to hold her in place, and there was no escape, nothing to do but stand still and let him kiss her with devastating thoroughness.

Her eyelids fluttered closed, blotting out the faint light, blotting out everything but the feel and taste of him. It was terrifying, it was smothering, it was dangerously splendid. She wanted to kiss him back, but she hadn't the faintest idea how to go about it. She wanted to lift her arms and touch him, but she was afraid to. He had his mouth on hers, his hand behind her head, but otherwise he wasn't touching her. And yet she felt captured, possessed, yearning, and she started to sway toward him, wanting that heat and strength tight around her.

He pulled away abruptly, taking a step back. She wrapped her arms around her body, suddenly cold, and lifted her eyes to look at him.

His breathing was slightly rapid, his mouth was damp, but apart from that he appeared completely unmoved. "You kiss like a virgin," he said flatly.

It was probably meant to be an insult. Instead it simply frightened her. Now wasn't the time for Reilly to discover she wasn't who he thought she was. Not with Timothy out of reach and the place crawling with soldiers.

"I don't like kissing," she said. A complete lie. As devastating as it was, she'd found her first kiss to be downright wonderful. She wanted him to kiss her again.

"That's a shame," he drawled. "It's a lost art."

I'm Caterina, she reminded herself, trying to hold on to her fast-fading self-control. "Perhaps," she said coolly, trying to sound suitably sophisticated. "I've never learned to appreciate it." True enough, she congratulated herself.

"Perhaps I could give you lessons."

She backed away from him, unable to hide her instant panic. Reilly didn't miss it—he wasn't a man who missed much—but he said nothing.

"I don't think so," she finally managed to say, pushing her short-cropped hair away from her face. "And I don't see why we have to share a room. Didn't the owner say this place was empty right now? Surely I could have my own room?"

Reilly's smile was cool and fleeting. "Sorry, princess. You're staying with me. Those weren't just any ex-soldiers lounging around downstairs, propositioning you. I made sure you couldn't see them and they couldn't see you, but I imagine you recognized their leader's voice."

"I don't know what you're talking about," she said, no longer caring if he guessed the truth.

"Well, maybe you wouldn't be that likely to run into your stepfather's chief executioner. He didn't run in the same social circles. That was Endor Morales, sweetheart. Quite possibly the most dangerous man in all of San Pablo, and it was just our dumb luck to run smack into him."

She fought back the panic that threatened to overwhelm her. "Do you think he suspected anything?"

"Morales didn't get as far as he did by being a trusting soul. He suspects everything and everybody. But as far as Dutchy knows, I'm just a low-life expatriate, probably a drug runner, with no interest in San Pablo politics. Morales won't be able to get anything else out of him, though I imagine he'll try. At lest the baby's out of the way, and we can probably manage to keep him a secret for a few hours. Long enough for a decent night's sleep and then get the hell out of here."

"Can't we leave now?"

"No way. Morales and his men will be watching us like hawks. Any change in our plans would set off alarm bells. We said we were going to spend the night, so we'll spend the night."

"But the baby..."

"The baby will be safe enough. The Shumi will keep him out of everybody's sight, and we'll be out of here first thing in the morning. For the time being all we can do is sit tight."

She looked up at him. "I'm afraid."

"Don't be. Morales didn't seem any more than casually interested. As long as you stay close you'll be safe enough."

"I'm not sleeping with you, Reilly!"

"Stop sounding like an outraged virgin," he said wearily. "Your honor, such as it is, is safe with me."

That was the second time in as many minutes that he'd called her a virgin. If she pushed it, he might begin to realize there was an unexpected truth to his accusation. He'd already turned his back on her, moving to the front of the room to stare out into the streets, dismissing her, and she told herself he wasn't interested. His kiss had been nothing more than another intimidation tactic.

"Am I allowed to take a shower alone?" she demanded frostily.

"Unless you want me to wash your back?"

She couldn't tell from his voice whether he was being facetious or not, but she decided not to push it. "When can I see the baby?"

He turned. "Keep away from the kid. He's as safe as he can be, and having you come waltzing around will just put him in danger. Dutchy's out of gas, and so is the damned jeep. He's supposed to get a shipment in the next day or two, so if Morales and his men have gone, it would be worth our while to wait. Otherwise we'll have to head out on the river. Or by foot."

"I think I'd prefer to ride," she said faintly.

"I imagine you would. Don't hog all the hot water. Assuming there is any," he added. "I wanted a shave, as well." He rubbed a hand over his bristly jaw.

"Don't do it on my account."

"Honey," he said wearily, "this is all on your account. If you hadn't run off from Billy and then decided to come back when things got a little hairy, neither of us would be in this mess. You'd be safe and sound in the States, the baby would have a nanny and you wouldn't have to be bothered with worrying about the little kid. You'd be out partying.''

''I doubt he'd find a better nanny than the Shumi women,'' Carlie said. ''And I don't like parties.''

''Since when?''

She shut her mouth. She wasn't made for deception. She wasn't made for hostility, she wasn't made for men, or kisses. And yet here she was, trapped smack-dab in the middle of it all. Unable, and unwilling, to escape.

''Take your shower, Carlie,'' he said, turning back to the window, dismissing her. ''I'll be here when you come out.''

''Is that supposed to be reassuring?''

''You'd better believe it. Unless you'd rather take your chances with the soldiers downstairs?''

''What's the difference?''

He turned to look at her. ''If you don't know, then I'm not going to bother explaining.''

For a moment she didn't move. He was a big man, tall, lean and strong. The stubble of beard on his chin, the dark amber eyes, the rough contours of his face suggested power and danger. And yet she trusted him. More than she ever thought possible.

The gun was tucked in the waistband of his khakis. It was a big gun that fit his big hands. It would keep her safe. It would keep Timothy safe.

"I know the difference, Reilly," she said, her soft voice an apology. She grabbed her knapsack and shut the door behind her, heading in search of the bathroom.

But behind her she heard the slow, savage curse of a man pushed to his limits. And she wondered why.

Chapter Seven

There was no question about it—she was making him crazy. There was no escape, either—with Dutchy prowling around, his piggy eyes suspicious, alert for ways to make an easy buck, he had to keep up pretenses. Not to mention that small band of Mendino's Black Shirts downstairs, complete with Butcher Morales watching over them. It wouldn't take much for them to come after Carlie, even without knowing who she was. She was female, she was pretty and he was the only thing that was stopping them. If they decided they could take him, it would be her death warrant. And it wouldn't be a pleasant way to die.

He glanced over at the bed. It barely qualified as a double, and that concave middle would roll their bodies together despite their best efforts. Maybe he should just say the hell with it, give in to temptation and have her.

Despite her maidenly airs, he knew perfectly well he could. Hector Mendino's daughter was notoriously easy, and she needed him. Add to that the look in the back of her eyes when she glanced his way, when she thought he wouldn't notice. She wanted him, all right.

It was neither conceit nor imagination that told him so. It was his instinct, honed over time, that hadn't failed him yet.

He sank onto the bed, the springs screaming in protest beneath his big frame. At least the place looked relatively clean, and the sheets smelled like sunlight. He wondered what it would be like to sleep beside Carlie's shower-fresh body, on sheets that smelled of sunlight.

The notion was dangerous. He could always spread his bedroll on the floor, though the scarred wood promised to be a lot harder than the packed jungle earth. He'd found Billy's wife in a convent—it would be suitably penitential for him to sleep on the floor.

The very notion of Our Lady of Repose still unnerved him. He'd always made an effort not to fall into that mind trap so many men, particularly those who'd been raised Catholic as he had, were prey to. Some thought women fell into two groups, whores or Madonnas. But in reality, life was never that orderly or convenient.

He liked women, he truly did. He liked their looks and their bodies, the foreign way their minds worked, the crazy way their emotions worked. He liked their laughter and their tears, their husky little cries, their feel and their scent and their taste.

But for so long there'd been no room in his life for anything more than the briefest of relationships that he'd almost forgotten how much he did like them.

And now was a hell of a time to be remembering. Trapped with a small, slight yet tough young woman who'd made his best friend's life a living hell. A woman who couldn't be further from what he wanted or needed. A woman he seemed to want and need anyway.

He heard a noise out on the street, and he wandered over to the window. Morales and his men were making a great show of leaving, something that failed to reassure him. He expected they wouldn't be going far.

There was no sign of Dutchy sending them on their way, another oddity. A man like the old innkeeper would be more likely to send his powerful customers off with admonitions to stop in again. If Dutchy wasn't downstairs, then he was somewhere else.

Reilly could move very fast, very quietly, even in heavy boots. He could hear the sound of the shower from the end of the darkened hall, hear Carlie humming beneath her breath. He paused for a moment, alone in the darkness, picturing her. What would she look like beneath the shower? The water sluicing down over those small, firm breasts of hers, breasts that had never nursed a baby. Her belly would still be soft from the pregnancy, her waist still thickened. The kid was less than a month old—it was amazing she'd had so much stamina. His sisters had been in a state of exhaustion when his nieces and nephews had been a month old, and they'd had all the benefits of modern life. Besides not having to trek through a jungle.

For a moment the thought of his older sister Mary, she of the placid disposition and the taste for sloth, being on a forced march through the rain forests of San Pablo brought a rare smile to his face. One that vanished when he heard a tiny knocking noise from the bedroom next to the shower.

The door was ajar. He pushed it open silently, and his night-trained eyes focused on Dutchy, his fat face pressed up against the wall, staring avidly through a narrow crack that let in a shaft of light.

The rage that filled him was immediate and overpowering. Dutchy never knew what hit him. One moment he was pressed up against the wall, drooling over the inhabitant of the shower room, in the next he was flat on his back on the floor, with Reilly kneeling over him, his big hand wrapped around Dutchy's wattled throat.

"Get a good eyeful, Dutchy?" he demanded in a harsh whisper. "I could make you very sorry you decided to play Peeping Tom with my woman."

"Hey," Dutchy gasped, "I didn't mean no harm. I was just looking, is all. Do you know how long it's been since I've seen a white woman around here? A look doesn't do any harm, and I didn't figure you for a possessive guy."

"You figured wrong. I'm very possessive," he said, increasing the pressure just slightly. Enough so that Dutchy's tiny eyes began to bug out even more, and he clawed at Reilly's arms uselessly. "Mess with me or my woman again, and you'll get more than a warning."

He released him and rose. Dutchy immediately curled up into a fetal ball, gasping and choking, cursing as he fought to regain his breath. A moment later he managed to stagger to his feet, stumbling out of the room, falling against the doorframe as he went.

The sound of the shower was still going. Carlie probably hadn't heard a thing. For that matter, Dutchy probably hadn't seen a thing. He'd been waiting for Carlie to finish, so he could watch her as she dried off.

He stood very still for a moment, in the darkened room. He could still feel Dutchy's neck beneath his hands, still feel the burning contempt that had washed over him, combined with an irrational, possessive rage. There was no reason for him to feel possessive. She wasn't his, and she never would be.

He needed to walk out of that room and slam the door behind him. But the crack in the wall let a narrow sliver of light into the room, and it called to him, with a siren lure.

He could think of any number of reasonable excuses. He needed to know just how much Dutchy had seen, so he could decide whether to poke his eyes out or not. He needed to look and see how strong she really appeared to be, whether she could withstand the rigors of the remainder of the journey. He needed to look and make sure she hadn't collapsed in the shower, oblivious to the scuffle in the other room.

He needed to look and remind himself that she wasn't the kind of woman he desired, that he didn't like small, trim bodies. He liked statuesque blondes, built along generous lines. He and Billy had been alike in that, though Reilly had always preferred his women to come equipped with brains, as well.

He needed to look and see what Billy had fallen in love with.

Damn it, he just needed to look.

There was no shower curtain. The shower was a rusted-out metal stall with a drain at the bottom, and Carlie stood beneath the stream of water, face upturned, oblivious to everything but the pleasure of the water sluicing down over her.

She was small, just as Reilly had suspected. Small, firm breasts, narrow waist, flat tummy. Smooth, creamy skin, beaded with water.

He backed away, furious with himself. Furious with the adolescent surge of desire that threatened to knock him to his knees. He was no better than Dutchy, a horny old man drooling over a naked woman.

He'd seen enough naked women in his thirty-six years to take one in stride. She wasn't the skinniest, the curviest, the shortest, the tallest, the ugliest, the prettiest. So why was he having this inexplicable reaction to her?

Jungle fever. Not enough food, not enough sleep. Hell, he needed a drink. Pushing away from the wall, he headed into the hallway in search of that very thing. Only to run smack-dab into Carlie, wrapped in an enveloping towel, hair and eyelashes spiky damp with water.

He looked down at her, keeping his expression cool and distant while he took into account that this towel was much thicker than the one he'd first seen her in. He couldn't see the shape of her breasts beneath it. But then, he didn't need to. He could remember quite vividly how they'd looked, taut with water streaming down around them.

"I take it you like prancing around in towels," he drawled. "Billy never told me that about you."

Even in the dimly lit hallway he could see her flush. "I didn't bring any clean clothes with me," she said. "What were you doing in that room?" She glanced over at the empty bedroom.

"Catching a Peeping Tom. Our friend Dutchy was watching you take a shower."

She clutched the towel even tighter around her slender body. It would be easy enough to take her hands, move them away and pull the towel off her. He could pull her into his arms, wrap her legs around his waist and carry her back to the room. And he had no doubt that Caterina Morrissey would let him.

"What did you do to him?"

"Let's say he won't be making that mistake again for a long time," Reilly drawled.

"What about you? Did you look?"

He gave her his best, most cynical smile. "What do you think, princess?"

"I think you're a pig," she said fiercely.

"Now that sounds more like the Caterina Mendino I've heard about," he drawled. "Did you save me any hot water like I asked?"

"No."

"Just as well. I think I'm needing a cold shower about now." And he sauntered past her, with just the right amount of swagger.

CARLIE WANTED TO KILL HIM. A white-hot surge of anger whipped through her veins, and she shook with the effort to control it. She didn't like anger. She wasn't used to strong emotions, love or hatred, desire or spite. She'd been in his company for less than forty-eight hours, and already she'd been through a lifetime of emotions. And each time she felt something fierce and implacable, it was harder to draw her hardwon serenity back around her.

She slammed the bedroom door behind her and pulled on clean clothes. It was marginally cooler that night, and the oversize white T-shirt disguised her lack of a bra. The loose cotton skirt hung low on her hips, brushing her ankles, but she took comfort in the feel of cloth against her legs. She wanted to be back in the safety of her cell, in the safety of her habit. This world was strange and unsettling.

Reilly was strange and unsettling. But he was the only safety she had left in her life, at least for now. She could make it through the next few days, long enough for him to get the baby safely out of the country, on his way to his grandparents. And then she would tell him the truth, make her way down to Rio de Janeiro with the sure knowledge that she'd been tested, most thoroughly, and risen above temptation. Surely Reverend Mother Ignacia could no longer deny that she had a calling, that she was ready to take her vows.

She moved to the window, running a hand through her short, damp hair. It was dark and quiet out there, only the occasional bark of a stray dog, the call of a jungle bird, piercing the humid night. She leaned her head against the wall, staring.

She missed Timothy. His quiet little sounds, the warmth of his small body against her. She knew with complete conviction that he was well taken care of. Yet she couldn't ignore the small, empty ache in her heart.

It would be worse, of course, when they got out of the country. Reilly would take him away, up north, to the big, soulless cities of the United States, and she would most likely never see him again. He would have grandparents to love him, and he would never even know about Sister Mary Charles, so important a part of his life for such a short, sweet time.

She heard the door open behind her. "You ready for dinner?" Reilly asked casually.

She made the mistake of turning to look at him. In the dim light of the oil lamp she could see him far too clearly. He was wearing a towel, and nothing more, and she had no illusions he'd done it purposely. Though there was no reason that he'd think a woman like Caterina Morrissey de Mendino would be discomfited by the sight of a man dressed in nothing but a towel.

But Sister Mary Charles was. She stood there, momentarily transfixed, staring at him.

His long black hair was wet, pushed away from his angular face, and he'd cut himself shaving. She'd known he was a big man, but without clothes he seemed even more massive. Not that his shoulders were immense, or his muscles bulky. He was lean and wiry and powerful looking, like no other man she'd ever seen. Dangerous and beautiful, he was like a jaguar she'd once glimpsed beyond the walls of the convent. Sleek and hard and mesmerizing. And she wanted to touch him.

"Close your mouth, Carlie," he murmured. "You'll catch flies."

She closed her mouth, still staring. He had a very tempting mouth himself. Wide, mocking, narrow lipped and sensual, it curved into a mocking smile at her trancelike state. "Better close those beautiful blue eyes of yours, as well," he added. "I'm about to get dressed."

She whirled back to the window just as he began to reach for the towel at his waist. She could feel the color flood her body, and she could only thank God the room was dark enough that he wouldn't see her embarrassment.

She stood there, staring mindlessly out the window, listening to the sound of clothes rustling. The snap of elastic, the rustle of cotton, the unnerving rasp of a zipper being pulled. That zipper told her she was now safe from future embarrassment, and she started to turn back.

He was directly behind her, dressed, thank God, though he hadn't bothered to snap the faded jeans he wore, and he'd left the khaki shirt loose and unbuttoned, bringing his smooth, bare chest unnervingly close. "Even your ears are blushing," he said, reaching out and pushing a damp strand away from her face.

There was a shattering tenderness in the gesture. She didn't want tenderness from this man, from any man. "Why would I blush?" she said in what she hoped was a suitably offhand voice. "I've seen hundreds of naked men."

"Besides which, if you're going to prance around in nothing but a towel, you're going to have to expect me to follow suit," he murmured. He was no longer touching her, but he was dangerously close. She could smell the soap on his skin. Toothpaste on his mouth. Danger in the air.

"I wasn't prancing," she said in a strangled voice. "And I wasn't blushing."

"You've spent too long at that convent," he said, closer to the truth than he'd ever know. "Some of the sisters' modesty must have worn off on you."

She stiffened. If she had any sense she'd ignore him. But she wasn't feeling very sensible. "Are you accusing me of trying to entice you?" she snapped.

"Not likely. You've been giving off that touch-me-not look for days now. I would have thought Caterina Mendino would have been more interested in cementing her right to protection, but you seem to take my nobility for granted."

"You'll protect me for Billy's sake," she said, certain at least of that.

"Wrong." He touched her again, with both hands this time, pushing her damp hair away from her face.

"You won't protect me?" Her voice wavered slightly. It wasn't the fear of his withdrawing his protection. It was the feel of his long, hard fingers on her skin.

"Yeah," he said. "I'll protect you. But not for Billy, and not for the baby. Not for the sake of those beautiful, lying blue eyes of yours." He ran his fingers across her cheekbones, and her eyes fluttered closed for a brief, dangerous moment.

"Then why?"

"Because I don't like to see the bad guys win. I don't like bullies, I don't like it when weaker people get hurt."

Her eyes shot open. "Who says I'm weak?" she demanded.

"Oh, you're not. Not in spirit. But a strong man could snap your neck in an instant. If you pushed him far enough. And you're a pushy broad."

The notion was so bizarre she had to smile. Meek, gentle Sister Mary Charles was a far cry from a pushy broad, but as long as he believed it, so be it. But one more thing was troubling her.

"Why do you say I have lying eyes?" she asked, wishing he'd take his hands from her face. Afraid of where else he might put them.

That cynical smile broadened. "They look so innocent. So sweet, and honest, and shy. But I know damned well Caterina Morrissey de Mendino doesn't have a shy, innocent bone in her body. You're a barracuda, lady. You may not look the way Billy described you, but I imagine your soul is just as twisted."

This was dangerous ground. About the only thing she had in common with Caterina was dark hair. Caterina had been tall and shapely, even in the advanced stages of pregnancy. Her eyes had been brown, Carlie's were blue. Her feet were big, her manner imperious, her tastes extravagant.

She raised her eyes and looked at him, for a moment hiding nothing. "Maybe you should believe my eyes," she whispered, "and not what you've heard."

He stared for a moment, unmoving, his hands cupping her upturned face, and she wondered if he'd kiss her again. Instead he backed away, suddenly, as if he'd looked into the face of a bushmaster. For a moment he looked dazed, and her sense of disquiet grew.

She lifted a hand to call him back, but he'd already turned from her. "I'll find some food for us," he said brusquely. "If I were you I'd stay put. I put the fear of God into Dutchy, and Morales and his men have left, but I don't trust them to have gone that far."

"What about the baby?"

"I'm going to check on him right now. In the meantime, sit tight. It's not safe around here, and I'm not in the mood to play hero."

"You don't really have the right qualifications," she said sharply.

He paused by the door, buttoning his shirt. "Oh, yeah? I would have thought I'd be perfect hero material. I'm big, a number of women have told me I'm handsome, and I fight on the side of law and order."

"You're a conceited oaf," she said, shocked at herself.

"Now you, on the other hand, don't quite qualify as a damsel in distress. You're too strong, and you lie too much."

There it was again, that trickling of unease. One she quickly squashed, as she realized he was about to abandon her in this Spartan hotel room. "Can't I come with you? I want to make sure the baby's all right."

"You can stay put. I'm going to check out a few other things while I'm at it, and I don't want you trailing around behind me, getting in my way."

"I can be very quiet...."

"No," he said, his voice sharp. And he closed the door behind him before she could utter another protest.

She stared at that door, remembering. She'd promised to do as she was told, no questions asked. She needed to keep that promise, to sit on the bed and wait until he deigned to return. She needed to ignore her empty stomach, her anxiety, her curiosity. She needed to remember the vows she wanted to take. Vows of obedience. Poverty. Chastity.

But she hadn't made those vows yet—Mother Ignacia hadn't let her. And she certainly had made no vows of obedience to Reilly.

Nor vows of chastity, either. She wasn't going to sit alone in that room, in the middle of the bed she'd be sharing with him, waiting for him to return. She was hungry, she was edgy, she was out in the world, for a short, dangerous time.

She wasn't going to spend that time cloistered in a hotel room as if it were her cell.

She opened the door and went after him.

Chapter Eight

Blue eyes, Reilly thought. Innocent, lying blue eyes, staring up at him. With a soft, tremulous mouth that needed to be kissed. Blue eyes, and a firm, slender body, with small, high breasts.

Billy Morrissey had had blue eyes, as well. Two blue-eyed parents, and the tiny baby Carlie carried strapped to her slender body had eyes that were already turning brown.

His knowledge of genetics wasn't that exact, but he somehow doubted that two blue-eyed parents would have a brown-eyed child. So who was the real parent? Carlie? Or Billy?

It made sense that Caterina Morrissey de Mendino had lied about the father of her child. After all, the Morrisseys were wealthy Americans who could provide a decent home for a baby. The real father could be anyone—a decadent member of the jet set Caterina used to pal around with, or one of her stepfather's bodyguards. Or anyone in between. No, her estranged husband was the most convenient choice, and whether he was anywhere near San Pablo ten months ago probably didn't matter.

He could hardly blame her. She was doing what was best for the baby, and if that included lying to everyone, so be it. He could find a certain grudging respect for a mother willing to risk it all for her child.

There was only one problem with that scenario. She didn't have the body of a woman who'd given birth less than a month ago. She might love that baby with a fierce, maternal passion, but she certainly hadn't given birth to him.

Of course, there could be any number of reasons for her masquerade. She could enter the United States as the widow of a citizen, but as the mother of a U.S. citizen, as well, her residency would be assured. She'd also have claim to the Morrissey money, which would be hard for anyone to resist. Chances were she was some friend of the real Caterina's, with the same expensive tastes.

Odd, he thought, moving silently through the shadowed street toward the Shumi encampment. She looked a lot younger than Caterina should have been. A lot more innocent. It must be part of her stock-in-trade. Along with an indefinable ability to make people want to believe in her. And he, the cynic of all time, was finding it far too easy to believe in her, as well.

Which all went to prove he'd been right in getting out. Not re-upping when his last tour of duty came to an end, heading out for his mountaintop in Colorado, away from danger and distractions. Whether he wanted to admit it or not, he was marginally more vulnerable than he liked. He had to be, falling for a lying little tease.

Except she hadn't kissed like a tease. One thing was for sure—she was lying to him, lying through her teeth, and he intended to find out the truth. In that small, concave bed tonight, he had every intention of finding out exactly who and what she was.

He'd be gone a couple of hours. He'd check on the kid, though he had no doubt Timothy was in the lap of baby luxury among the Shumi women, then he'd scout out the village, quietly, assessing the danger. That should give Carlie just long enough to start worrying whether he was coming back or not. Just long enough to panic and be ready for the slightest bit of extra pressure.

Oddly enough, he didn't find the notion appealing. He didn't want to scare her. Didn't want to terrorize her into telling him the truth. He wanted her to offer it, freely.

Another sign of dangerous weakness, he thought with disgust. If he wasn't careful he'd end up as dead as Billy Morrissey. And he wasn't quite ready to die.

The night was still and marginally cooler than the heart of the jungle they'd just traversed. The slow-moving river that ran through the village was deep and brown, the currents sluggish, but he thought he felt his first hesitant breeze since he'd landed in this miserable country. The heat, the rebels, the murderous black-shirted soldiers, the presence of Morales himself, the jungle, all added up to dangers that were scaring the hell out of him. The sooner he got those two out of here and safely back to the States, the sooner he could retire to his mountain and pull himself together.

Oddly enough, he had no hesitation about taking them both back. One of them didn't belong, maybe both of them. It didn't matter. He wasn't going to leave a helpless baby in this war-torn country, not when he had the means to get him out. And whether Carlie had given birth to him or not, she truly loved him. He was sentimental enough to figure that counted for something.

In the distance he heard the faint scream of a jaguar, deep in the jungle. And like a great jungle cat himself, he slipped into the shadows, on the prowl.

IT DIDN'T TAKE CARLIE long to regret her decision to follow Reilly. Even though the old building seemed deserted as she tiptoed downstairs, she could feel eyes, watching her. Male eyes, hungry eyes. She'd felt those eyes on her ever since she'd arrived at this place, she admitted to herself.

The bar downstairs was deserted, thank God, the soldiers gone. She took a good look around through the murky lamplight. Cigarette smoke still hung in the air like a noxious cloud, and she could smell whiskey and chiles. The latter made her stomach growl in longing.

Surely someone like Dutchy would employ a cook. The Shumi were noted for their cooking as well as their family values—with any luck there'd be someone in the kitchen, eager to feed her.

Luck, however, was not with her. The kitchen was nothing more than a back shed, the stove was cold, the stores almost negligible. There was a bowl of eggs of doubtful vintage, a hunk of hard cheese, some plantains. And three cans of Campbell's soup.

She stared in disbelief. She had forgotten the existence of canned soup. Centuries ago, when she'd lived in the States, it had been a major part of her sustenance. Looking at those red cans, she could suddenly remember her mother—vague, preoccupied, opening a can with the assurance that this would provide a decent meal for a growing girl. She could always taste the toast and butter.

It seared through her with a sharp pain. Memory. Grief. Shock. She thought she'd put that all behind her, found a safe new life with the sisters, protected from harsh, unbearable time. And just as easily it came rushing back, simply by looking at a can of soup.

She was shaking all over. She could smell the blood once more, pooling beneath the beating sun. The screams were gone, but the shouts of the soldiers still echoed. They were searching for her—they knew she was somewhere in that mountain village, and they weren't about to leave a witness behind. And she'd backed down, curled into a fetal ball, and waited for them to come and finish her.

But they'd never found her. She'd been brought out safely, that time of horror locked safely away in the back of her brain. It had been so long since she'd even thought about it.

Until Reilly had dragged her back into life. And the memories came flooding back as well, crushing her.

She couldn't let it crush her. With sheer force of will she thrust the panic, the despair away from her. This time she couldn't curl up in a weeping, helpless ball on the floor, waiting for someone to rescue her. She had a vow, to Caterina, to the baby, to herself, even if Mother Ignacia wouldn't let her make a formal vow. She would see Timothy safely into his grandparents' arms, and she would return to the sisters. There the past would safely recede, and she would find peace once more.

She reached for the can of soup, ignoring the tremor in her hands. It took her a while to find the can opener, longer still to use the rude contraption. And then she sat on one of the stools, took a spoon and began to eat out of the can, the cold salty stuff a far cry from the warm comfort her mother had provided her so long ago.

The stale corn bread didn't taste anything at all like buttered toast, either. And yet she knew the flavors. It felt oddly like a kind of communion. Bread and wine. Cold soup and corn bread. In remembrance of her mother.

Would Mother Ignacia call it blasphemy? Perhaps. But to Carlie it felt like a sacrament. Remembering. And letting go, just a tiny bit.

"You eat my soup?" The heavily accented voice was deep with outrage.

Carlie looked up to see Dutchy standing in the doorway. He was a large, untidy man, with blood-shot eyes, several days' growth of beard that didn't look the slightest bit raffish, a pot belly and a stained, rumpled white suit. His gray hair stood up around his bald spot, and he glared at her for a moment, his small dark eyes cunning.

"I'm sorry," she stammered. "I was hungry, and I couldn't find anything else. We'll pay for it...." Belatedly she wondered if Reilly had any money with him. Of course he did—he was infuriatingly efficient.

Dutchy pushed into the room, an expression of false affability crossing his lined face as he pulled out a cigar. "No, no," he said grandly. "You should have let me know. I could have had one of the Shumi cook you something. A pretty girl like you shouldn't have to eat cold soup out of a can." He cast a sorrowful look at the empty container, the spoon still sticking out of it.

"It reminded me of my childhood." She said it on purpose, testing herself. There was no pain. Not at the moment.

"That's why I keep it around. To remind me of civilization while I'm in this godforsaken place. It's very hard to come by."

"And I took one. I'm sorry."

Dutchy moved closer, the cigar smoke wreathing around him like an anaconda. "For a pretty little girl like you," he said, breathing heavily, "I don't mind. Where's your friend?"

"He just went out for a walk. He'll be back at any moment." Alarm coursed through her, immediate, justified. There was no other exit to the kitchen shed. Just the door Dutchy was blocking. She slid off the stool, trying to summon up a cool smile. A Caterina, to-hell-with-you smile.

"That's right," Dutchy cooed, coming closer. "A nice, friendly smile. You be nice to Dutchy, and he'll be nice to you. Morales and his men haven't gone far, and they're coming back. They wondered about you, and your friend. They'll wonder even more about the baby you left with the Shumi women. You shouldn't expect to keep secrets in a place like this. The Shumi won't talk, but others will. And I've promised to report anything unusual to Morales. He wouldn't like it one bit if I held out on him."

"What baby?" she demanded, unable to hide her panic.

"Don't be foolish. I found out, and so will Morales. But if you're nice to me, and you play your cards right, I can keep them away from you."

She backed away from him, surreptitiously, but he followed, until she was up against a wall, nowhere to run to, and he was far too close, his big belly pushing up against her, his cigar smoke wreathing them both. "You be friendly to me, little one, and I can be very helpful. People around here know that Dutchy is a good friend to have." He reached out a hand to touch her face. His fingers were short, stubby, stained with dirt and nicotine, and as he brushed them against her cheekbone she couldn't control her horrified shudder.

Dutchy's grin widened, exposing dark, broken teeth. "You like that, do you?" he murmured, completely misinterpreting her reaction. "You're a woman of discernment. Broad shoulders and a handsome face are all well and good, but there's a lot to be said for age and experience." His hand slid down the column of her neck, and her skin crawled. "Give me a little kiss, sweetheart, to show your good intentions."

He leaned forward, his belly pressing against her, his hand groping at her breast, and there was no escape.

She stood motionless, terrified, defenseless, ready to suffer and endure, when a cool, mocking voice interrupted them.

"Messing with my woman, Dutchy?" Reilly stood in the doorway, a silhouette in the shadowy light. "I thought you were smarter than that."

Dutchy backed away from her so quickly it would have been comical. But Carlie was in no mood to laugh. She realized she'd been holding her breath, and she let it out, wondering if she was going to throw up all over Dutchy's filthy white suit.

The old man was already across the kitchen, hands raised in the air in a defensive gesture. The fact that Reilly was pointing a gun at him probably encouraged his attitude. "I meant no harm, Reilly. I'm just a harmless old flirt, you know that. I can't let a pretty girl go by without making a pass at her. No need to point that gun at me—it was all in fun."

"Was it?"

His voice was grim, deadly. Carlie stood there, mesmerized. The sight of the gun in his strong hand brought back other memories, other hands holding guns, and the nausea rose farther in her throat. "He didn't hurt me, Reilly," she said, silently pleading with him to put the gun away.

Oddly enough, he did, tucking it back into the waistband of his jeans. "Lucky for him," Reilly murmured. "Get out of here, old man."

Dutchy left, almost tripping in his haste to escape, and they were alone in the tiny shack. She'd thought it was crowded with Dutchy bearing down on her. It was nothing compared to Reilly towering over her, looking dark and disapproving.

"I thought I told you to stay in your room," he said.

"I was starving," she said, squaring her shoulders and trying to pull some of her self-control back around her. She still felt shaken, frightened, helpless. She didn't like that feeling. Any more than she liked realizing that Reilly's presence was rapidly banishing that fear, replacing it with another, more disturbing kind of tension. "I didn't know when you were coming back."

"So you decided to come exploring. Were you looking for a meal, or a better offer? Morales may have been *el presidente*'s chief enforcer, but all that ended when your stepfather was assassinated. Those soldiers are renegades. Your stepfather's dead, Caterina, and those loyal to him have gone their own way. You're nothing more than a pawn now."

"I wasn't—"

"As for Dutchy, I think you already discovered exactly what he's interested in. He's a bigger danger than an anaconda, and if you think you can trust him—"

"I don't trust him!" she snapped. "I was hungry, I told you."

He looked at the empty can of soup. "You must have been desperate," he said calmly. "You want anything else, or are you ready to go up to bed?"

His even tone of voice was deceptive. She looked up at the big dark man, and fear was back. "I want my own room," she said. "My own bed."

"I'm sure you do. But you wouldn't get it. You can share with me, you can trust me, damn it," he said, suddenly angry. "Or you can start out the night alone. You wouldn't end up that way. Either Dutchy or one of Morales's men would be joining you."

"I can take care of myself."

"Sure you can. I just had a perfect example of just how good you are at protecting yourself," he drawled.

"I could have handled him," she said, knowing just how unlikely that was.

"Maybe you could have. But I'm not going to risk Billy's kid's life on that slim chance. You do as I say, no questions asked, and we'll be out of here before they even know we're gone."

"Are you really that confident?" she asked faintly.

"I'm really that good."

There was nothing she could say to that. It wasn't a boast, it was a simple statement of fact. And she believed him.

"All right," she said. "I won't argue with you."

"That'll be the day," he drawled, half to himself.

"I don't argue!" she said, shocked.

"Lady, you have a very cantankerous streak when you forget you're trying to convince me you're a Madonna."

He probably thought he was being funny. The words cut her to the quick, though, bringing into doubt almost anything she'd ever believed about herself. "What do you mean by that?" she demanded.

"I mean there seem to be at least two people inside that small, luscious body of yours. There's the saintly mother of the year, trudging along behind me, following orders, biting her tongue, peaceful and serene and not really of this world. Then there's the strong, angry young woman who gives as good as she takes, who questions authority and who's driving me crazy. And somewhere in all that mess is Caterina Morrissey, a spoiled, self-absorbed tramp. I'm just trying to figure out which one is the real you."

"Who told you Caterina Morrissey is a tramp?"

"Honey, I read the letter you wrote Billy. Where you told him you were having a better time sleeping around the continent and you didn't feel like being the wife of an American soldier, even a rich one. Kind of put me off a bit, I do admit."

There was nothing she could say. She could remember Caterina's weak, hesitant last confession. A confession that was neither sanctioned by the church nor forgiven by the holy rites, but a confession free and honest and true nonetheless, between two unlikely friends.

"I'm not going to argue ancient history with you," she said instead, primly. "I'm ready to go up, but first I'm dying of thirst. That condensed soup was pure salt. Is there anything to drink around here?"

"This is a bar, Carlie. There's plenty."

"I was thinking of water."

"We'll save any decent water for the baby. You can make do with beer."

"I don't drink—"

"You'll drink beer and like it. Your other choices are so potent I'd end up carrying you and the kid for the next three days. I could do with a couple of beers myself."

By the time she followed him back into the bar he'd already pulled the caps off two tall dark beers. She took one from him, looking at it askance, but he was ignoring her, tipping the bottle back and pouring it down his throat with obvious enjoyment.

She had no choice in the matter—she was so thirsty she could go out and suck a cactus. She took a big gulp of the lukewarm stuff.

It tasted strong, dark and yeasty. She drank half of it, then wiped her mouth. "It's good," she said, half in surprise.

"The princess doesn't usually deign to drink beer?" he drawled.

"Not this kind." It was an easy enough lie.

"Funny, I would have thought Dos Equis would be just your style."

She drained the bottle. "Is there another one around?"

His mouth curved in a smile. She liked his mouth, she decided. It was one of the reasons she trusted him. "Here you go, princess."

"Don't call me princess," she snapped.

"Ah, the bitch is back."

She choked on the first gulp of beer. "I beg your pardon?" she said, glaring.

His smile was positively beatific. "I think I like you best this way," he said, taking her arm and herding her toward the stairs. "I suspect it's the real you."

"I want another beer," she said, hanging back.

"You haven't finished that one."

She pulled away, stumbling slightly when he let her go, and drained the second bottle. "There," she said triumphantly.

He just looked at her. "I thought you were used to drinking."

"I am."

"Not from the looks of it, kid. Two beers is the cheapest drunk I've ever seen in my life. I heard you used to be able to pack it away like a professional."

Dangerous ground, she thought hazily. "Maybe my metabolism changed since I gave birth."

"Maybe," he said. "Think you can walk upstairs?"

"Don't be ridiculous," she snapped, full of dignity, staring past him. The floor was slightly unsteady, and she reached out a hand to balance herself. Unfortunately he was the one she reached for.

If she'd felt dizzy before, it was nothing compared to being swooped up in Reilly's strong arms. Ascending the steep staircase didn't help the woozy state of her brain, either.

"Could you take it a little slower?" she murmured, sinking back against him, totally incapable of fighting him at that particular moment. "I'm dizzy."

"Don't worry, princess," he drawled. "The night is young. I'm not about to let you go to sleep."

"You're not?" She tried to summon up a latent wariness, then gave it up.

"Not until you answer a few questions."

They were in the upstairs hall by now, and it was very dark. She wondered hazily where Dutchy was now. If he'd gone after the soldiers. "I answered all your questions, Reilly."

"Oh. I just had a couple more." He kicked open the door to the bedroom, his voice deceptively affable. The oil lamp had burned down low, sending out only a small pool of yellow light.

"Such as?"

He carried her over to the bed, and she found herself strangely loath to let go of him. There was a strange glitter in his eyes, one she couldn't read, and his mouth was dangerously close. She wondered what he'd do if she kissed that mouth. She wanted to try it again. She'd liked her first attempt, liked it very much indeed. She imagined she'd improve with practice, and the amount of beer she'd drunk made her feel pleasantly warm and eager to try again.

"Such as who the hell you really are," he said softly. "And whose baby you're trying to pass off as your own."

Chapter Nine

Reilly wondered, quite calmly, whether the young woman in his arms was about to throw up on him. She looked green, her huge blue eyes were stricken and her body, even in this humid night air, felt tense and cold.

"You're crazy, Reilly," she said, but her voice shook.

He considered dropping her on the bed. He didn't want to—a dangerous reluctance he was willing to acknowledge, even as he deplored it. He didn't want to let go of her at all, but he knew the longer he cradled her against his body, the harder it would be. In more ways than one.

He put her down, gently enough, and took a step back, away from her. She made the very grave mistake of not staying put. She scrambled off the bed in a panic, the beer she'd drunk making her awkward. It was child's play to catch her by the door, pulling her back around, against him. Child's play to look down into her frightened, upturned face, and exert the last little bit of pressure.

"Crazy?" he replied in a low, menacing drawl. "I don't think so. I don't know whose baby that is that you've been playing devoted mother to, but it's not yours. You didn't give birth a month ago. I don't think you've ever been pregnant in your life."

"What would you know about it?" she demanded furiously. Another mistake on her part.

It was a simple enough matter to push his hand up under the loose white T-shirt she wore, to cover her small, perfect breast. She tried to jerk away in shock, but he held her tightly, allowing no escape. And then she held very still, looking up at him in mute despair, as his hand cupped her breast and the peak hardened against his palm. "I watched you in the shower, remember?" he taunted her in a low voice. "Babies wreak havoc on a body, especially one as small and slight as yours. Your breasts would sag, whether you were nursing him or not. The skin on your stomach would be loose, your waist would be thick, your stamina would be shot to hell. I don't know whose baby you've been cooing over, but it's not yours."

"You're crazy," she said again, trying to disguise the panic in her voice, and failing. "Timothy is mine and Billy Morrissey's, and you can't prove otherwise."

"Oh, yeah? What color were Billy's eyes?"

Her hesitation was so imperceptible he found he was impressed. "Hazel."

"Wrong. It was a pretty safe guess, though. I'll grant you that. Billy's eyes were a bright, bright blue. You have blue eyes yourself, princess. The baby's eyes are already turning brown."

He pulled her a little closer against him. He knew he ought to release her breast, but the feel of its small, mounded warmth against his palm, the hard nub of her nipple, the way she shivered in his arms, were all too delicious to resist. He was very hard, and he didn't mind her knowing that as well, as she stood plastered up against him. There was no way she could miss it, and yet she still seemed slightly disoriented, confused by him and her own body. Maybe those two beers had had an even greater effect on her than he'd originally thought.

"Whose baby?" he said again, softer now, arching her back slightly. "Does Caterina Morrissey have brown eyes?"

Her body slumped in defeat. Against his. "She had brown eyes," she said in a low voice. "She's dead."

"I thought so. But Timothy was hers?"

The woman nodded. "She died soon after he was born. It was a massive infection—there was nothing I could do. I could only promise that I would make sure Timothy got safely out of this wretched country."

Release her, he told himself. He loosened his grip marginally, but she made no effort to escape. He considered whether he could flatter himself into thinking she was starting to like it, but he didn't think so. She was simply too dazed to realize her compromising position.

If he had a speck of decency he'd let her go. She was ready to spill—he didn't need to use any sort of physical intimidation on her anymore to pry the truth from her. But the feel of her warm, smooth skin beneath his hand was irresistible. He wanted to cup the other breast, as well. He wanted to lean down and taste it.

"So he really is Billy's baby. His grandparents will be pleased to hear that. Why didn't you tell me the truth?"

"I did. You didn't believe me."

He nodded, remembering. "So you did. I guess I'm a little too used to liars. So who are you, if you're not Caterina Morrissey? And how did you end up at that deserted convent?"

Sudden awareness darkened her eyes as she realized her position, plastered up against him, his hand on her small, perfect breast. She wrenched herself away and he let her go, disguising his unwillingness. She sat back on the bed, keeping her face averted, but he could see the unexpected color on her cheekbones. Just as he recognized her rushed breathing, and her nipples pressing against the thin cotton of the white T-shirt. Her ladyship was turned on, and she either didn't know it or didn't like it. Maybe a combination of the two.

"I told you, I was a friend of Caterina's. My name really is Carlie. Short for Caroline. Caroline Forrest."

"How did you and Caterina become friends? She tended to fly with a pretty rich crowd. And what were you doing at that convent?"

"I was taking care of Caterina."

"Why?"

She looked up at him, her blue eyes wide and slightly dazed. She was about to lie to him. He recognized that fact with a combination of irritation and triumph. If she continued to lie, then all bets were off.

There was no reason he should play the little gentleman with a liar.

"Because no one else would," she said. "All the nuns had left. I... I've known Caterina for years. We were in school together, in France, and we used to have fun together. She wrote me a few months ago and asked me to come visit. I thought we were going to continue to party when I came to San Pablo."

"You picked a lousy time for a vacation. Don't you read the newspapers? Don't you have the faintest idea of the political upheaval around here?"

"There's political unrest everywhere," she said with a brave attempt at a shrug. He was impressed. If he didn't already have reason to distrust her he would have believed that shrug. She looked up at him defiantly, and she would have convinced most people she was simply a spoiled party girl, caught in the middle of a revolution.

It would be easier on him if he did believe it. He could take full advantage of that small, trim body that had such a surprisingly potent effect on his, and if she was who she said she was, she'd be more than agreeable.

Dutchy had been scared off. Morales and his men were well out of reach, at least for now, the baby was safe and the door was locked. He looked at her, taking in the brave defiance in her pale mouth, and pulled the gun out of his waistband.

Her eyes followed that gun, nervously. She'd had a bad experience with guns in her life, he could tell that much. If he were a real bastard he could use that gun to make her tell him the truth this time. Not that half-baked lie of French finishing schools and the like.

But he put the gun down on the table beside the bed, close enough so he could reach it if someone decided to interrupt them, and then moved closer to her. Her eyes were at the level of his zipper.

"All right," he murmured. "I'll believe you. What do you want from me?"

"I want Timothy to be reunited with his grandparents."

"And you'll accept safe transportation to the States, as well," he drawled cynically.

"I'm not sure."

Another lie, though this didn't sound like one. She wanted to get the hell out of this country, back to the same cushy life Caterina would have had. "Oh, I imagine you'll decide soon enough, princess," he said. "Tell me, were you going to tell anyone the truth? Or were you going to keep passing yourself off as Caterina Morrissey?"

"Caterina Morrissey wasn't exactly a recluse," she snapped, some of her anger struggling back. "Plenty of people would know I'm not her."

"Good point. Besides, I imagine you have family somewhere, who wouldn't take kindly to your up and disappearing."

"I have no family left." She didn't look at the gun lying on the table. She didn't need to. In certain ways she was a mystery to him. In certain ways she was far too clear.

"All right. Let's get your story straight," he said, moving around to the other side of the narrow bed and dropping down, lightly. She jerked, but she had enough sense not to leave the lumpy mattress.

"I don't need to get my story straight," she said irritably. "It's the truth. My name is Caroline Forrest. I'm twenty-six years old, American, an old school friend of Caterina Mendino's. My family's dead, and I came to visit Caterina at the wrong time, that's all. She asked me to keep her company during the latter part of her pregnancy, and I agreed. When her stepfather was killed we arranged to go to the Sisters of Benevolence, and we stayed there for the last two months. Caterina gave birth, she died soon after, but she asked me to make sure her baby was taken care of. She said Billy would be coming for them. But instead you showed up."

"And the rest is history," he said, stretching out on the bed and eyeing her. "Of course, there's no way to check it. Caterina, and Billy, and almost everyone else who would know the truth are all dead. The good sisters have deserted San Pablo, and that just leaves you and me and the baby."

"You'll have to trust me."

"Why should I?"

"Because I trusted you. Enough to come with you."

"But not enough to tell me the truth," he said. "Okay, I'll believe you."

She was gullible enough to take him at his word. More proof that she wasn't part of Caterina's decadent crowd. She gave him a hesitant smile. A dangerous one. For both of them.

It would be simple enough to find out the truth. And more temptation than he felt like resisting at that particular moment. "That means we don't need to worry," he said in a deliberately low voice.

"Worry about what?"

"About whether you can do it or not."

"Do what?"

There was no coquetry in the question. He almost hesitated, but he wasn't in the mood for hesitation. He slid his fingers along the back of her neck, threading them through her short-cropped hair, bringing her close to him. She didn't resist, but her eyes were wide and dark and frightened.

"Do what?" he echoed mockingly. And he told her, in precise, Anglo-Saxon words. In detail. Exactly what he wanted to do to her.

He was totally unprepared for her reaction. He expected coyness, or even enthusiastic participation. She moved so fast, jerking away from him, that another man might have let her go.

But Reilly was in fighting form, in the midst of a war-torn country with the enemy surrounding him, and two people dependent on him. His reflexes were automatic, hauling her back across the bed so that she lay across his body, trapped, panting, staring at him with terror and something else indefinable in her eyes.

"I didn't say I was going to rape you," he said irritably. Though he wasn't sure why he should be so mad at himself. He'd set out to test her, to scare her. He'd succeeded in what he'd wanted, hadn't he?

Except what he wanted was her mouth. Her panicked blue eyes closing as he kissed her. He wanted her small, perfect breasts against his bare chest, he wanted her strong, pale legs wrapped around his hips. He wanted her strong hands with their short, unmanicured nails digging into his shoulders. He wanted to make love to her.

"No," she said. Her voice wavered just slightly, her only sign of fear.

"Who are you saving it for, princess? It's a long night, and who knows where we'll be tomorrow? We're sharing a bed, we might as well share the rest of it, as well."

"No," she said. She was still half lying across his lap, his unmistakable erection.

He slid his hand behind her neck, pulling her closer. She didn't resist, and there was resignation in her eyes. Resignation, and anticipation.

He kissed her then. Her mouth opened beneath his, willingly enough, though she jerked in surprise when he pushed his tongue past her lips. He held her still, his large hand cupping her neck, and she quieted after a moment. Letting him kiss her. Making no effort to fight him. No effort to kiss him back.

He lifted his head and looked down at her. "Practicing passive resistance, Carlie?" he murmured. "I told you, I'm not going to rape you."

"Then what are you doing?"

"Just satisfying my curiosity." He released her, and she moved to her side of the bed as quickly as she could. She didn't try to run again. She already knew he could catch her.

He leaned back against the lumpy pillows, watching her. "I'll make a deal with you, Carlie," he said lazily. "Kiss me back, and then tell me no. And I'll believe you."

Her blue eyes were clouded, wary. "You think I won't be able to resist you? Your conceit is really extraordinary, Reilly."

"I didn't say that. Just kiss me as if you mean it. And then tell me no. And I promise I won't touch you again."

She moved very fast, as if she didn't dare stop to think about it, swiveling around and pressing her closed lips against his, hard. Slamming his lips against his teeth, jarring his head, banging his nose, before she pulled back, obviously shaken.

He sighed. "You can do better than that," he said. "Kiss me as you'd kiss a lover. Or I'll kiss you."

As a threat it was hardly that devastating, but she reacted with unflattering fear. He waited, patiently enough, stretched out on the bed, and this time she considered it.

"All right," she said, getting to her knees, the long skirt swirling around her on the bed. He wondered whether she was wearing anything underneath it. He didn't think so, and the thought made him ache.

Unfortunately he'd made a bargain with her. And he had every intention of keeping his side of it, as long as she kept hers.

She tilted her head to one side, as if considering how to go about it. Leaning forward, she put her small, strong hands on his shoulders, and brought her face up close to his. He watched her through lowered lids, but there was no mistaking the indecision and panic in her eyes.

"What are you afraid of, Carlie?" he murmured, his voice low and hypnotic. "It's just a kiss."

She closed the distance between them and put her mouth on his. Lips still closed tight over her teeth, her hands gripping his shoulders, she kissed him like an early Christian martyr going to the stake.

She pulled back, but he reached up and covered her hands with his, holding her there. "You can do better than that," he taunted her. "Use your tongue."

He half expected her to argue, but instead she put her mouth against his again. He reached up and cupped her face, stroking the sides of her mouth with his thumbs, and her lips softened, opened against his. He lured her tongue forward, carefully, masterfully, rewarded with her tentative touch against his, the quiet moan of pleasure that came from the back of her throat. Her mouth was sheer delight, hypnotizing, innocent, like nothing he had ever tasted before, and the desire that was raging through his body rose to new heights as he deepened the kiss. He teased her, taught her, and she responded with growing delight, moving closer, her breasts within reach, her hands clutching his shoulders now, her eyes tightly closed, her mouth open, seeking, seeking....

In the distance there was the sound of gunfire. She tore herself away from him, scrambling back across the bed, but this time he let her go.

She looked at him as if he were the devil incarnate. He simply leaned back and managed a cool, deceptive smile. She had to know what was going through his body, but he wasn't about to belabor it. "You were just beginning to get the hang of it, Carlie. It's hard to believe you were part of Caterina's crowd of high-living jet-setters."

"I told you, I don't like kissing," she said.

"You could have fooled me. You seemed to be developing a definite affinity for it." He stretched back and closed his eyes, waiting.

It didn't take long. "Is that it?" she demanded, sounding uncharacteristically exasperated.

He opened one eye. "Is that what? I presumed the answer was still no. If you changed your mind..."

"The answer is still no."

He smiled sweetly. "Then good night."

She stared at him, baffled. It was something of a consolation. He would have found a great deal of satisfaction burying himself in her small, gorgeous body, but without her cooperation he'd have to settle for second best. Driving her crazy.

She sank down beside him, turning her back in a furious huff. Unfortunately the nature of the bed didn't allow for temperamental snits. She slid up against him on the concave mattress.

She immediately tried to scramble away, clinging to the side of the bed. "You aren't going to have a very comfortable night like that," he observed, sitting up and watching her.

"I don't anticipate having a comfortable night as long as you're around," she snapped.

"You're forgetting, I'm the one who's keeping you alive," he said lazily, reaching forward and turning down the oil lamp until the room was a dark cocoon. "If I hadn't gotten back, you'd be in Dutchy's bed, whether you liked it or not. And he probably has fleas."

Silence. "Thank you for saving me," she muttered. Belated. Grudging.

"My pleasure," he replied, glad the inky darkness hid his grin.

She wasn't falling asleep. The bed practically vibrated with her tension, and he wondered whether she was going to be fool enough to try to sneak off when she thought he was asleep. He deliberately relaxed his body, changed his breathing, to see whether she'd go for the bait.

"Reilly?" she whispered after a long moment.

He said nothing, waiting to see whether she'd slide off the bed and try to make it to the door.

But apparently escape wasn't on her mind, not at that point. "Reilly," she whispered again. "What are you going to do with me?"

"Keep my hands off you."

"That's not what I meant. I meant—"

"I know what you meant," he drawled. "And the answer hasn't changed. I'll take you where you want to go. To the States, if you want, or the closest safe airport outside of San Pablo. I'm taking the baby to his grandparents, but I'll make sure you're safe, as well."

"Even though I lied to you?"

"Even though you lied to me."

"And what do you want in return?" She sounded her usual distrustful self, and he allowed himself a weary sigh.

"I thought I made that clear. Nothing that you aren't willing to give. Now go to sleep, Carlie."

"But—"

"Go to sleep, or I'll give you another lesson in kissing. And I might even manage to change your mind."

She didn't make another sound. The tension in her body gradually began to lessen, and in less than ten minutes she was sound asleep, her small, sweet butt pressed up against him.

He only wished he could find a similar oblivion.

Chapter Ten

Her dreams were shameful. Lascivious, shocking things, the likes of which hadn't bothered her for years. She'd worked so hard at banishing dreams from her life. The terrifying nightmares that brought back full force the bloody day when her parents had died. The lustful dreams that left her feeling hot and trembly. Even the peaceful dreams, where God seemed to be speaking to her, had been blocked from her life. She would wake up once they started, jarred into consciousness and safety.

But she must have been too tired to fight it. The big, strong body stretched out beside hers, touching hers, worked its own insidious effect on her, invading her defenses, her longings, her dreams.

Her skin was hot. Prickling with awareness. There was a strange gnawing sensation in the pit of her stomach, and her mouth ached. In her dreams she knew she'd been wrong. She'd kissed a man. She'd taken pleasure in it, she who'd eschewed men and this world. And she wanted him to kiss her again.

Concrete images faded, to be replaced by shifting patterns, sensations. Heat and dampness, flesh and muscle, bone and sinew, taste and desire. She was running then, down a long hillside, chasing something that she couldn't quite see. And he was behind her, waiting for her. She had only to stop, to hold out her hand, and he'd pull her back, away from the pit filled with noisy, cawing blackbirds, their wings flapping, their white veils fluttering in the jungle breeze....

Her eyes flew open in sudden awareness. She was lying pressed up against Reilly's body, the thick darkness all around them, with only the soft glow of moonlight sending a faint light in the room. Her arms were around him, tight, and it was more than clear that she'd crawled over to his side, crept up to him while she slept, looking for comfort, looking for something she was too big a coward to define.

His eyes were open, still, in the moonlight, but he made no move to touch her. She found she was clinging to him, and he let her. Beneath her hands, beneath the thin cotton T-shirt he wore, she could feel the beat of his heart. Steady, slightly fast.

"You were dreaming," he said.

"Yes."

"Nightmares. About guns and death."

"I do sometimes," she said, too weary, too vulnerable to protect herself by lying. She was too close, and the heat and strength of him were irresistible. She knew she should apologize, move away. She knew she couldn't.

"What happened?"

Another time she would have been more wary. She would have remembered the story she'd been telling him, about the privileged life of French finishing

schools. But she was still half-asleep, still shaken from
the vivid dream, and she wanted to tell him what she'd
never told another living being.

"They killed them," she whispered, her head down.
She could feel the wetness of tears on her cheeks, and
she pressed her face against the soft T-shirt, the hard,
warm skin beneath, letting the soft cotton soak up the
dampness.

He was holding her, loosely, comfortingly, one hand
smoothing back her short hair. "Who did, Carlie?"

She tried to resist. "I don't want to..."

"Who did?"

She couldn't fight him, and herself, and her need to
tell him. "The soldiers," she said, her voice barely
discernible. But she knew he heard every word. "They
came to Puente del Norte and they killed them all. My
parents. The people in the village. Even the children."

"Why didn't they kill you, Carlie?" His voice was
a soothing rumble beneath her tear-streaked face, and
the large, rough hand kept stroking, stroking.

"They couldn't find me. I was hiding, behind a
clump of trees. I couldn't move. I couldn't even hide
my head. I just had to stay there, and watch, and...
and...listen...."

His arms tightened around her then. For a brief
moment she fought it, but he simply held her, his voice
that same comforting rumble. "There's no one to hear
you, baby," he murmured. "No one to see you. No
one to know if you cry."

"I'd know," she said.

His hand slid beneath her hair, tilting her face toward his. "You already know."

He took her breath away. She wouldn't have expected him to have an idea of her torment, and yet he'd honed in on it immediately. And there was no way she could deny the truth of his words.

"I . . ." she began, one more token protest. But her voice failed her, and she began to cry. Noisily. Wetly. Burying her face against him once more, howling out her misery and rage, her loneliness and pain. She cried until her stomach ached with the force of her sobs, cried until her eyes stung and her chest ached and her nose was running with no tissue in sight. And all the while he held her.

He was an astonishing man. When her storm of tears began to fade, a bandanna appeared in front of her. She pulled away from him with no more than a quavery sigh, wiped her face, blew her nose and looked at him defiantly.

His T-shirt was damp from her tears. His face was hidden in the shadows, but she imagined she could see the gleam in his eyes, the faint grimness to his mouth.

"Reilly," she said, hardly recognizing her tear-roughened voice.

She wasn't sure what she expected from him. Questions, mockery, a pass. She wasn't sure which she'd hate the most.

She'd underestimated him. He simply lay back on the bed, looking at her out of steady eyes. "Are you ready to sleep?" he asked. "We've got a long day tomorrow."

She wasn't sure what she should do. She was embarrassed, self-conscious.

He solved the problem for her. He caught her arm and pulled her back down beside him. Up close, pressed against him. He draped an arm over her, a possessive, protective arm. And then he closed his eyes, obviously prepared to go to sleep.

She held still, barely daring to breathe, overwhelmingly conscious of the heat of his body, the warmth of his breath against her hair, the steady thump of his heartbeat. It thumped at deliberate counterpoint to hers, and she tried to match his breathing, but hers was lighter, faster, as if she'd been running. Punctuated by the remnants of her bout of tears.

Odd, that she could feel so comfortable and so uneasy at the same time. She wasn't used to touching other people, and the feel of his body plastered against hers, the casual possession of his arm, made her feel threatened.

And yet, she felt safer than she ever had. This was a man who would protect her, no matter what. This was a man who'd watch out for her, for the baby, who'd do what he said he would do, and nothing or no one would stop him. He was stubborn as a mule, but she realized for the first time in almost ten years that she wasn't frightened of the future.

And she wasn't frightened of the past.

She should have told someone, anyone, the story of what she'd seen in that tiny mountaintop village. The horror had been so real that she'd wanted to shut it out, and she'd been afraid that by talking about it she'd somehow make it real, give it power over her.

Not realizing the power it had already claimed.

She could have told Reverend Mother Ignacia. She could have confessed to Father Ramon, not any real sin, but the miserable guilt of surviving when so many had died. But instead she'd buried it in her heart, where it ate its way into her soul like a worm, until it came pouring out, confessed to a man of violence not that far removed from the men who had committed those atrocities.

And yet he was. Just because he carried a gun, because he was willing and able to kill, didn't mean he was one of them. He looked out for the innocents of this world. For Timothy. And for her.

"Reilly," she said, her voice husky and still in the darkness. She half expected he'd be asleep already—he didn't strike her as the sort of man who let a little thing like sleep disobey his command.

But a moment later he answered. "Yeah?"

"Thank you."

"For what?"

"For scaring Dutchy off. For bringing us out of the jungle. For letting me cry all over you. For putting up with me...."

"Don't get maudlin on me, princess," he drawled as his long fingers gently stroked her bare shoulder where the loose top had slipped down. It was a simple gesture, meant no doubt to reassure. So why did it strike a hot spark deep within that dark, evil part of her? Why did it make her want to move closer still, to wrap her body around his and soak up his strength, his heat, his very being?

She froze, terrified at the rush of longings surging through her. She needed to get away from him. He was seducing her simply with the force of his presence, seducing her away from the safety she'd longed for and worked for. And he didn't even want her.

She needed to be strong. She needed to remember her priorities. Get the baby safely out of the country, on his way to his grandparents. And then join Mother Ignacia and the others, older but wiser.

"If you don't relax," Reilly whispered in her ear, "I'm going to figure out a way to tire you enough to make you fall asleep. Right now I can only think of one way to accomplish that, and while it seems like a fine idea to me, you've already said no. So if you want me to respect your wishes, you'll stop wiggling around and sighing. Unless you want that wiggling and sighing put to good use."

Carlie froze. He breathed a loud sigh and began to rub the tight muscles in her back with his strong hand. She tried to will herself to go limp, but she simply couldn't. Not surrounded by the heat and the scent and the feel of him.

"All right," he said in sudden exasperation. And before she knew what was happening he'd spun her over, onto her back, and he was straddling her, his big, strong body covering hers. "We'll do it my way." And he covered her mouth with his.

She struggled, but it was useless. He was so much bigger, so much stronger, so much more determined. Mother Ignacia had counseled her about rape. When they had first brought her to the Sisters of Benevolence she had scarcely been able to speak, so deep was her shock, and for the first few months it had been assumed that she had been raped. Even when part of the truth came out—that she was from a village destroyed by war—Reverend Mother was very matter-of-fact about the dangers of living in a country where their faith and their habits sometimes couldn't protect them. She had escaped, physically unscathed. There was no guarantee her luck would continue.

It was no sin, Reverend Mother had said. When faced with rape, don't put your life in danger, trying to fight. If you can't escape, submit. God has already had enough martyrs.

Submit, she reminded herself, lying stiff and straight as a board beneath him, waiting for his hands to paw at her. It would be over soon enough. Perhaps this was the price she had to pay for her sins, to suffer this base degradation....

Except it didn't feel like degradation. His mouth danced across hers with the lightness of a butterfly, brushing against her tightly closed lips. He held her pinned with his body, but with one hand he began pulling the loose cotton shirt from the waistband of the skirt. His warm hand was on her waist, sliding up to cover her breast, and she squirmed, trying to buck him off.

She might just as well have tried to dislodge a boulder. He was slow, deliberate in his caress of her breast, and she opened her mouth to cry out in protest.

He slid his tongue inside her mouth. She arched again, but it seemed to push her breast against his rough-skinned hand, and the sensation was... disturbing.

Not nearly as disturbing as what he did next. He rolled to his side, taking her with him, and her skirt was bunched up around her thighs. And his hand was between her knees, sliding up toward the center of her being.

Submit. She heard the words in her head again, but she couldn't make them echo in her heart. She didn't want to lie back and let him do this, she didn't want him to break his promise. She had trusted him—if he took her by force he would prove himself no better than Morales's men, or Dutchy. He just happened to smell better. And taste better. And feel better.

As she realized the way her mind was going, she panicked. Submission was all well and good, but not if she was going to enjoy it. There was no way Reverend Mother would countenance that.

She hit him, catching him on the side of the head with her fist. He barely seemed to notice. He simply caught her flailing arms with one strong hand, pinning them to the sagging mattress beneath them. And he pushed his other hand up under her skirt, between her legs, where no one had ever touched her before.

It was shocking, it was sinful, it was disgusting, it was ... Carlie's eyes fluttered closed for a moment as he touched her, intimately. A faint shimmer of pleasure danced along her nerves, and her eyes opened again in outrage.

"Relax, Carlie," he murmured. "It's better than a sleeping pill."

She tried to jerk her hands free, but he was too strong. She opened her mouth to protest, but he simply put his own mouth over hers, as she let him kiss her, knowing it was wrong, unable to help herself.

She was wet between her legs. His hand was making her wet. It astonished her, as the tremors and trills of reaction amazed her. She considered begging him to stop, but she knew that would be a waste of time. She considered praying for deliverance, but quickly ruled that out. She didn't want to be delivered. Besides, the sinful, wonderful feelings that were lashing through her body were entirely incompatible with the stern God she'd followed for the past nine years.

His mouth left hers, trailing across her cheekbone, but she could no longer fight him. It was too late—her will, her honor had been sapped. He had no right to do this, no right at all, holding her there, forcing her...

"Let it happen," he said in her ear, a deep growl. "Stop fighting it, Carlie. You want it, you need it and I can give it to you. Just let it come."

She had no idea what he was talking about. She was cold, and hot, her brain had ceased to function and her entire body was racked with tremors. She wanted to cry out but she couldn't, she wanted to hit him, she wanted to put her arms around him, but her hands were trapped, her mouth was silenced by his, her body was imprisoned, and there was nothing she could do beneath the sleek, devilish onslaught of his hand between her legs, his fingers pushing deep inside her innermost being, his thumb pushing, pressing, sending shards of shimmering delight through her.

And then it happened. One moment she was trembling in helpless reaction to the terrible things he was doing to her, in the next her entire body convulsed. Releasing her hands, he shoved her face against his shoulder, muffling her hoarse cry, but she was beyond noticing. Blackness closed in around her, a timeless, deathless eternity, shot with a pinprick of stars dancing in front of her eyes, as everything stopped, her heart, her breathing, the world on its axis.

It lasted forever. And then she was suddenly dropped back, into reality, into the small, stuffy room at the edge of the tropical jungle, lying in bed with a professional soldier, her skirt up to her waist, her blouse shoved up to her armpits, her entire body a shaking, quivering mass of exhaustion.

Now he was going to do it, she thought distantly. He was going to rape her, and she couldn't bring herself to argue, or to care. She felt as if she'd run twenty miles, and her entire body was so limp she let her eyes drift closed, content to just let it happen.

He pulled her skirts back down around her legs with gentle hands. He pulled the shirt back down, as well. He stretched out beside her, pulling her up close to him, and she was too weak to do anything but curl up next to him. Now he'd hurt her, she thought sleepily. Now he'd force her.

And within moments, she was sound asleep.

REILLY LISTENED to the sound of her deep breathing with a mixture of amusement and exasperation. He'd accomplished just what he'd set out to accomplish, by force, no less. If a small, selfish part of him had hoped she'd get into the spirit of things long enough to return the favor, he should have known he'd be squat out of luck. He'd been through a streak of purely miserable misfortune for the past year and a half, starting with his realization that he just couldn't hack the army anymore, his falling-out with Billy, followed by Billy's crazy marriage and then his death. All ending up in this stupid trek through the jungle with a newborn infant and a woman who had no connection to either the Morrisseys or Reilly. A woman who didn't know how to kiss, seemed as out of touch with her own body as a puritan, and made him so damned horny he thought his insides would fall out.

How could anyone so small, so unpracticed, turn him into the human equivalent of Jell-O? He'd spent his entire military life following orders and giving them, but the bottom line had always been the most good for the most people. His priorities were very clear here. He needed to get Timothy Morrissey home to his grandparents. Carlie Forrest was just an unnecessary complication.

Her breathing was deep, even, drugged with sleep and satisfaction. The sound made him smile sourly. Lord, he was turning into a regular knight, rescuing damsels in distress as well as babies, and even providing safe sex when they needed a little cooling off.

But what about him? He could do with cooling off, or safe sex, or the hot, slick feel of her around him. And instead she fell asleep in his arms with as much trust as the third member of their odd little party.

The smart thing to do would be to leave her behind. She was good with the kid, but he could handle the little guy, as well. Timothy slept most of the time, drank formula, and Reilly had no problem with diapers.

What he did have a problem with was Carlie. More exactly, he had a problem with himself. She distracted him, and when he was distracted, they were all vulnerable.

He'd come too far, the stakes were too high, to risk everything because suddenly he couldn't stop thinking with his zipper.

She made a sound in her sleep. A wet, shuddering sound, a stray remnant of her crying jag. She'd seen her parents killed, she said. By the black-shirted soldiers of the San Pablo army.

Which was in direct odds with her story about making her first visit to San Pablo to visit an old school chum.

She'd been lying to him again, which came as no surprise. He could shake her awake, demand the truth from her and maybe precipitate a confrontation that would slake the burning thirst he had for her. Any excuse to touch her, to push her, to have her.

But he wasn't going to do it. Any more than he'd leave her behind for Dutchy's tender mercies. He'd find out the truth from her, sooner or later.

In the meantime, he'd indulge himself in the painful delight of sleeping with her soft, slight body pressed up against his. And he'd think of the look in her eyes when she came.

Chapter Eleven

"Fifteen minutes."

The words, gruff and abrupt, ripped through Carlie's sleep-dazed brain. Her face was pressed up against the pillow, and she was alone in the bed. However, the man she'd shared the bed with stood directly over her, and she wasn't particularly ready to face him after last night. Any more than she was ready to face herself.

She lifted her head, keeping her gaze on the pillow. The room was still fairly dark—only the faint light of sunrise pierced the gloom, sending mauvy-pink shadows against the cracked walls. "Fifteen minutes?" she echoed.

"We're meeting the Shumi down the river a ways. They'll be bringing the baby. Dutchy's passed out on the barroom floor, but when he wakes up I imagine he'll be going after Morales. We need to be long gone by then."

She still couldn't meet his gaze. "Why would he go after Morales?"

"Because I knocked the crap out of him. Because he got a good look at you and knew you weren't a camp follower. Because if he's heard about the baby he'll probably want to tell Morales about it. Don't forget about the reward. So the sooner we get out of here the better.''

''I can make it in five.''

''You've got time for a fast shower. God knows when you'll get another chance.''

She couldn't avoid it any longer. She turned her head to look in his general direction, still determined not to meet his gaze. It was a mistake. He was wearing jeans and nothing else, and his hair was slicked back from the shower. He was big and wet and dangerous, and yet far too familiar. His mouth, his hands had touched her. Caressed her. Turned her wanton.

''Stop blushing,'' he said irritably.

Of course, her blush deepened. For a moment, endless, eternal, her eyes met his. They were dark, brooding, filled with some latent emotion she couldn't begin to understand. She'd seen lust in the faces of men, seen it on Dutchy last night, but this didn't look as simple as lust. Besides, if he lusted after her, he wouldn't have stopped last night. He wouldn't have...done that to her, and then simply gone to sleep.

Though she suspected that she'd been the first to fall asleep. She'd lain there, waiting, and the next thing she knew it was morning, and she awoke feeling embarrassed, energized and achingly aware of life and all its possibilities.

''It's getting closer to ten minutes,'' he warned her.

She pushed back the covers. Her clothes were tangled around her, but she was still relatively decent once she yanked the skirt down around her legs. It wasn't as if he wasn't more acquainted with her body than any human being, herself included. But he'd only touched her body, not seen it, and she'd just as soon he didn't.

The room was small and the bed took up most of it. She skirted around it, grabbing clothes from the open backpack and heading for the door. He was standing there, watching her, too close.

She wanted to run. She wanted to scurry away like a small, embarrassed rabbit, and he probably knew it all too well. She paused beside him, squaring her shoulders and meeting his cool gaze. "Don't ever do that again," she said fiercely, despite her blushes.

It was a mistake. His dark eyes lightened with real amusement, and his mouth curved. "Don't do what?"

Her color deepened. "Just don't," she said in a strangled voice, wishing she'd had the sense to escape and keep her big mouth shut.

But she hadn't. He put his hands on her shoulders and pushed her up against the wall, gently, inexorably, his fingers kneading her. "Don't what?" he taunted again, softly. "Don't make you come? I thought I was a perfect little gentleman," he murmured, his mouth brushing against her ear, his breath tickling, disturbing her. "Ready to provide pleasure without asking a thing for myself." His mouth traveled across her cheekbone, down to the corner of her lips. "I thought next time I'd use my mouth."

If she turned her head, just a fraction of an inch, she could have kissed him. And the devastating thing was, she wanted to. She wanted his mouth covering hers again, taking, giving pleasure. She wanted him to push her back on that bed and show her that soul-shattering delight once more.

She started to tilt her head, to give him better access, when he whispered against her lips, "You're down to five minutes now."

She drove her fist into his stomach. Hard. He didn't even flinch. He simply backed away, his expression enigmatic. "Better hurry," he said, turning away from her.

He had a beautiful back. Long, graceful, with smooth, darkly tanned skin. She'd never realized a man's back could be quite so lovely.

"I'll be ready," she said tersely.

REILLY DECIDED it might be wiser not to be in the room when Carlie came back. Just as he resisted the temptation to join her in the shower. The sooner they got away from this little outpost, the better.

There was no sign of Dutchy when he reached the bottom of the stairs, and Reilly cursed beneath his breath. Last time he'd reconnoitered, Dutchy had been passed out beneath a table, snoring loudly, and Reilly had hoped his drunken stupor would last well into midmorning. Time enough for them to be long gone.

Apparently fate wasn't about to be so kind.

He could hear noise in the back shed that passed for a kitchen—the clanging of pots, the loud, muffled curse. He could move out of there without Dutchy knowing—Reilly was good enough at what he did to ensure that. But he couldn't count on Carlie, small though she was, being similarly light on her feet. Besides, he could hear the shower going overhead, and if he could, Dutchy could.

He had no real choice in the matter. He set the packs down wearily. He pulled the gun from his waist, checked the clip and then headed for the kitchen.

CARLIE WAS JUST PULLING on her clothes when she heard the sound of the gun. For a moment she didn't know what it was—she was still concentrating on not envisioning what Reilly had meant when he'd said next time he'd use his mouth.

All sorts of disasters flashed through her head when she finally realized just what that muffled explosion was. The worst was Reilly, lying dead in his own blood, murdered by Morales's soldiers.

She didn't stop to consider the safety of her actions. She was out of the bathroom, still buttoning the loose cotton shirt, and halfway down the stairs when she saw him.

Reilly stood in the darkened bar, whole and unharmed. He looked grim, shaken, but he looked up at the sound of her footsteps, and she thought she could see the dark despair in his eyes.

"I thought someone shot you," she said in a husky voice.

"No such luck," he said after a moment. He sounded weary beyond belief. "You're stuck with me."

Something was wrong. Something was terribly, terribly wrong. Carlie descended the last few steps, fighting the temptation to go to him. Touch him. Hold him.

"Is Timothy all right?"

He nodded. "I trust the Shumi. They should be waiting for us downriver." He moved to shoulder the two packs. "Let's get out of here."

"Where's Dutchy?"

"He won't be bothering us."

"Why not?"

He stopped beside her. He looked bleak and very, very angry. "Don't ask."

She looked at his hands, expecting them to be stained with blood. They looked no different. She looked up at his face, searching for the mark of death, the emptiness of a lost soul in his eyes.

But there was no difference. And little wonder, she reminded herself. He was a soldier, a man of death. This wouldn't be the first time he had killed in cold blood. It wouldn't be the last.

She followed him through the outlying jungle as the dawn lightened the sky, heading toward the muddy, slow-moving river, grieving. It wasn't that Dutchy was a worthy soul, but he was one of God's creatures, and he didn't deserve to be shot down like an animal.

But even more, she grieved for Reilly. For his lost soul, and the choices he made.

The sight of the baby, safe and smiling in a Shumi woman's dark arms, brought a measure of relief to her. She pushed past Reilly, rushing to the baby, and the majestic woman handed him over with a smile and a voluble conversation about his wisdom, his appetite, his sturdy limbs and the magnificent future such a young prince had in store for him. Surely with a strong, brave father like the Anglo and a good woman like her, he would be blessed throughout his life, and would enjoy the blessings of many brothers and sisters springing forth from their fruitful loins.

Carlie kept her back to Reilly, mentally thanking God he wouldn't understand the Shumi dialect. In a quiet voice she thanked the woman for her good care of her son, hoping Reilly wouldn't notice her conversant ability.

She should have realized that Reilly noticed everything. The Shumi woman launched into a frank, well-meaning discussion of exactly what Reilly and Carlie should do if they desired another boy, or how best to achieve a female offspring next time, complete with appreciative remarks about Reilly's no doubt remarkable proportions and skill as a warrior and a lover.

It was sheer force of will that kept Carlie from blushing this time. That, and the knowledge that at least Reilly didn't know what they were saying. And that he wouldn't understand her polite reply, promising that she would do her best to let him come at her from the back, with her hands over her head and nothing but a belt of gigua grass around her waist if she were interested in having twins.

"Your carriage awaits, milady," Reilly drawled.

Carlie turned, having composed her expression into one of polite interest. The politeness faded when she caught sight of the canoe. "We'll die," she said flatly.

"I doubt it. The Shumi have been using these for over a thousand years. They're small, but they're well made."

"Yes, but they know how to steer them," Carlie protested, holding Timothy so tightly he let out a soft little sound of protest.

"So do I. Get in." He'd dumped the packs in the center of the dugout, and there was another basket of fresh fruit and flat bread that was almost enough to entice Carlie into that barge of death. Almost.

"We're not going anywhere in that thing," she said flatly.

He looked at her, and she could feel the anger simmering in him, ready to snap. He was a man at the edge. She didn't know how she knew, she didn't know what had put him there, but with a sure instinct she knew she had to be very careful.

Perhaps it was killing Dutchy. Even a man as hard as Reilly might have difficulty murdering in cold blood. Maybe it was something else. She just knew when he spoke in a quiet, clipped voice that she'd better listen.

"You'll get in the damned boat," he said between gritted teeth, "or so help me God I'll tie you up and drag you behind us. There won't be much left of you by the time we get to our next stop, given the piranhas and the crocodiles that infest this river, but at least I wouldn't have to listen to your infernal yapping."

He took a menacing step closer, and it was all she could do to stand her ground, the baby clasped protectively against her.

"You'll do what I say." His voice was cold and dangerous. "If you think the baby's in danger on the river, let me tell you that the alternatives are far worse.

And the longer you stand about griping and moaning, the greater the danger is. Get in the boat.''

Carlie got in the boat. It tipped for a moment, then righted itself as she sank to the floor, cross-legged, the baby resting between her legs. She bit her lip, keeping her gaze forward, as she felt the solid weight of Reilly land behind her.

The Shumi waved them off, singularly unmoved by the battle they'd just witnessed. "Gigua grass," one of the women called after them in the Shumi language. "Have your man wear some as well, around his—"

"Goodbye," Carlie called nervously, interrupting the cheerful graphic instructions.

Reilly was right, of course. He did know how to handle the wide, slightly tippy canoe, and they slid through the water with surprising speed. Within moments they had turned a bend in the slow-moving river, out of sight of the Shumi.

"They'll be all right, won't they?" Carlie asked after a moment. "Morales and his men won't hurt them?"

"Morales and his men won't find them. The Shumi have twice their brains and half their bulk. They've had to deal with conquistadors and fascists. They know how to survive, how to disappear into the forest."

Carlie looked down at the baby's peaceful little face. "You promise?" she demanded.

Reilly began to curse. Colorful obscenities floated through the air, then were cut off with such abruptness that she turned to stare at him, sending the boat rocking dangerously.

"Life isn't fair, princess," he said flatly. "And promises aren't worth...squat. It's about time you learned that."

"But—"

"But nothing. You can't watch out for everyone. You can't save the world. You can concentrate on saving your own ass, and that's the way things work."

"Then why are you here?"

"Beats the hell out of me," he said.

The river was noisy that early in the morning. The birds were having an early gossip, the howler monkeys screeched to each other across the treetops, the somnolent river made its own steady sound as the boat moved with the current. Timothy slept in her arms, serene and replete, and Carlie leaned back against the stack of supplies, gazing skyward. It looked so peaceful, so far removed from blood and death, and unable to help herself, Carlie shivered.

"Did you have to kill him?"

Utter silence from the back of the boat. Then, "What the hell are you talking about?"

"Dutchy. Did you have to kill him?"

Reilly cursed under his breath, not quite loud enough for Carlie to make out the words. Another surprise—he hadn't minded cursing in front of her before. "I didn't realize you'd developed a fondness for old Dutchy. Maybe I shouldn't have gotten in his way last night."

"He was a horrid, disgusting old man," Carlie said fiercely. "But he didn't deserve to die."

"Trust me, angel, he more than deserved it. Dutchy's done more things, caused more harm than your vivid imagination could even begin to guess at. However, I didn't kill him."

She turned, and the boat rocked perilously. "I heard the gun," she said.

"I shot at him. It scared the living . . . it scared him, which was what I wanted. After that it was a simple enough matter to tie him and leave him in a back bedroom."

"Did you leave the ropes loose enough so that he could eventually escape?"

"Hell, no," he said irritably. "But Morales and his men will be back sooner or later, and they'll find him. If the snakes don't first."

"Reilly!"

"Don't worry, angel. Snakes are too smart to touch an old bastard like Dutchy. They wouldn't want to get poisoned."

"You wouldn't lie to me, would you, Reilly?"

"Lie to you?" There was something in his voice, a combination of amusement and irritation. "Now why would I do that? I don't like liars. Besides, isn't lying a sin?"

Alarm bells began to go off in Carlie's brain, but she carefully kept her face forward. "I wouldn't know," she said. "I don't spend my time thinking about sin."

"What about last night?" he taunted. "Was that a sin? Exactly what kind of religion do you follow? I presume you're Catholic, since you spent that time with Caterina and with all those nuns. If I remember my childhood catechism properly, there's a whole set of categories for each sin, isn't there?"

"I wouldn't know."

"Were they venial sins or mortal sins, I wonder?" he said, half to himself. "There ought to be some sort of grade of venial sins. I imagine kissing you was only a second-class sin," he murmured. "Touching your breasts would have been third class, making you come would have been bordering on major venial sin. But I imagine it would be a mortal sin if and when I actually did you."

"Reilly..."

"But we weren't talking about sex, were we? We were talking about death. I don't give a damn whether you believe me or not, angel. But the fact of the matter is, if I'd blown Dutchy away, as I was sorely tempted to do, you would have smelled him. Death is ugly, and death stinks to high heaven."

"Don't." It was a quiet moan of protest, one she doubted he'd listen to.

"You're right," he said. "I'd rather talk about sex."

Carlie clenched the sides of the boat. She heard the plop of water as a crocodile slid into the river, eyeing them out of beady little eyes. He started toward them, then seemed to think better of it, using his tail to swerve back, away from the small boat as it moved swiftly downriver.

"Too bad," Reilly murmured. "I was in the mood to shoot something."

"Where are we going?" Carlie asked somewhat desperately. "Do you have any sort of plan, or are we just wandering through the jungle, one step ahead of Morales and his men?"

"Don't forget the noble rebels. They aren't any too friendly, either. Fortunately they're to the south of us, and we'll be heading north, once we reach our next stop."

"What's our next stop?"

He seemed to consider it for a moment. "I suppose I'll trust you," he allowed.

"Big of you." She couldn't resist snapping back.

"After all, there's no one you're likely to tell. Caterina Morrissey de Mendino would have been out for her own tail, but I'm not so sure about Carlie Forrest. Besides, I don't intend to let you out of my sight."

"Reassuring."

"Isn't it, though?" he said with false sweetness. "We're heading due east to a small settlement called Cali Nobles. There's a small trading post there, run by a man named Simeon. A much better sort than our friend Dutchy. I can count on Simeon to find us some sort of transportation north."

"North?" She hadn't been in the hills north of San Pablo since the rescue workers had first taken her down out of the mountains. She didn't want to go back.

"That's where my plane is. If we're going to get out of here in one piece we need to get to my Cessna. Look at it this way, angel, at least you won't have to walk. Or do you have a problem with flying?"

"I haven't flown in years."

"Oh, really. Then how did you get to San Pablo to visit your old school friend Caterina?"

Damn him, she thought, savoring the first curse she'd uttered, mentally, in years. "By yacht, of course," she said serenely.

"Ah, yes, Transatlantic yacht. Remind me, Carlie. How long ago was that?"

"Two months," she said determined to bluff it out.

"And one more question," he said, paddling smoothly through the water.

"Yes?"

"Where do we find some gigua grass?"

Chapter Twelve

Carlie almost wished the trip downriver could have lasted forever. It was peaceful and quiet in the bottom of that little boat, with only the occasional whine of insects to disturb her calm.

Reilly seemed to be suffering from a massive case of the sulks, though she couldn't quite figure out why. He wasn't talking to her, which was just as well. She hadn't been able to come up with an answer to the gigua-grass question. Obviously he understood the Shumi language far better than she had imagined. He'd understood every word of the woman's cheerful advice on procreation, as well as her agreeable responses.

Fortunately the baby was growing more alert, and she concentrated her attention on him, talking in a low voice that she hoped wouldn't reach back to the taciturn Reilly. "Did you miss me, little boy?" she murmured. "I missed you. I know you must have liked being taken care of, not being jostled around all the time. It won't be too much longer before we get you home. You'll have a grandma and a grandpa to love you and take care of you, you'll probably have cousins and—"

"No cousins," Reilly interrupted from the back of the dugout. "Billy was their only child."

"Then they'll love you all the more," she assured the baby determinedly. "They're probably just waiting to dote on you, sweetie. Though I hope your grandma isn't too old...."

"Actually, the Morrisseys can afford the best of everything for their only grandchild. Including the best of household help. He'll be looked after by experts. And I doubt a high-powered Washington hostess like Grace Morrissey would care to be referred to as 'grandma.'"

She turned back to look at him, her concern for the baby overriding her determined avoidance of him. "They'll love him, won't they?"

"They sent me down here to get him, didn't they?" he countered irritably. "They were willing to foot the bill."

"They're paying your expenses?" she questioned, oddly surprised.

"No." He gave the paddle a harder push, sending the canoe skimming through the water. "I owed Billy that much, and more. It was the least I could do."

She turned back to the baby lying across her lap, looking up at her trustingly out of those surprisingly brown eyes. "They'll love you," she said firmly, loud enough for Reilly to hear. "Or your Uncle Reilly will beat them up."

Reilly's response was a muffled obscenity. "I'm not the kid's uncle," he protested.

"You told me you and Billy were like brothers."

"We grew apart. People change. We had a couple of arguments."

"Still, you came after his wife and baby. You must have forgiven him."

"There was nothing to be forgiven," Reilly said. "Just a parting of the ways. And don't try to make me out as some kind of good guy. I happened to owe him for any number of things. This gives me a chance to pay my debt."

"You don't owe me anything. Why are you taking me along if you're not a good guy?"

"You keep this up and I'll toss you to the crocodiles," he drawled.

"Sure you will, Reilly," she said, feeling suddenly, surprisingly cheerful. She looked down at the baby. "Your uncle's a liar, sweetie. Don't pay any attention to a word he says. He'll look out for you."

She could practically hear Reilly's temper simmer. It was a mildly entertaining diversion, to be able to annoy him so thoroughly, and these days she needed mild diversions. All this excitement was a bit too much for her placid heart to handle.

Though she was beginning to wonder whether her heart was that placid after all. She'd taken the danger and adventure with surprising equanimity, and she'd survived her first taste of passion without dying of shock.

Reverend Mother Ignacia had always been frank about the sins of the flesh. She had maintained that God had given them all bodies to enjoy, and there was nothing shameful about pleasure. To be sure, it was better sanctified by God and a priest, but a pragmatic woman had to accept that life didn't always work out so neatly.

She'd listened to Carlie's protestations that she had no interest in sensual matters, but she still refused to let Carlie take her final vows. Carlie was finally beginning to suspect why.

She'd never had any doubt about Mother Ignacia's wisdom and perception in other matters—why had she assumed that when it came to Carlie she'd suddenly lost her ability to see clearly?

Carlie leaned back against the supplies, gazing out over the slow-moving river. The baby dozed peacefully, and behind her she could feel Reilly's strong, steady movements as he propelled them through the water. It was a perfect time for reflection, to consider what she'd never dared consider before.

Perhaps, just perhaps, she'd misunderstood her calling. Perhaps she really had been hiding, from memories, from pain, from life.

She still wanted to hide. She wanted to be back in the safety and stillness of the convent, her body unawakened, her soul single-minded, her heart determined. There were too many choices out here. Too many distractions.

Including the innocent child lying in her lap, trusting in her to keep him safe, to love him. And including the not-so-innocent man behind her. What did he want from her? Anything at all? And what was she willing to give him?

The fear fluttered in her stomach once more, combined with a tightening lower down, a clenching of memory that came against her will, and she wanted to run.

But there was nowhere to run to. Not in this crazy, war-torn country, not while she needed his help to protect the baby. She just had to get through the next few days, till they got out of here. Then, away from his distracting presence, back in the shelter of the convent, she could decide what she really needed in life.

The thought should have soothed her. But somehow the idea of leaving this man, and this child, cut her to the heart, and she closed her eyes against the brightness of the tropical sun, and the sting of her own tears.

IT WAS A STRANGE and novel sensation for Reilly, this urge to wrap his hands around her throat and strangle her. He wasn't a man prone to violent fantasies; he simply did what needed to be done. If that need included violence, he would do it, without undue hesitation or recriminations.

He knew perfectly well why he wanted to strangle her. Dutchy was out of the way, but he'd been quite voluble once Reilly had fired that bullet close enough to crease his filthy suit. And he'd been mad and drunk enough not to consider the benefits of discretion.

"So how does it feel to pork a nun, Reilly?" he'd demanded blearily as Reilly had lashed him to the old iron bed with the filthy sheets.

"What the hell are you talking about?" he'd said, yanking the ropes unnecessarily tighter.

"Your little lady friend. I thought she looked familiar, but it took a while before it came to me. She came from the convent, didn't she? Our Lady of the Perpetual Virgin, or whatever it was, right? Bet she was real tight.''

He slammed Dutchy back against the bed, his hand around his wattled neck, ready to press the life out of him. ''You're crazy, old man.''

Dutchy wheezed in laughter, too drunk to realize his life was hanging by a thread. ''You mean she didn't tell you? I wouldn't have thought she could put anything over on you—you're getting soft, Reilly. It's no wonder you're getting out of the game.''

''You must have gotten into some bad whiskey,'' Reilly said between gritted teeth. ''That, or the jungle's finally gotten to you.''

''I even know her name,'' Dutchy said. ''She was the only young one there, and I make it my business to keep track of all the young white women in the area. Sister Maria Carlos. Her parents were those missionaries that were killed a number of years back. But what I can't figure out is where the baby came from.''

He pressed against his throat, just a bit harder. Dutchy's eyes began to bulge, and he gasped for breath.

Reilly timed it perfectly. Just until Dutchy passed out. Then he stepped back, watching him, and he realized he was shaking.

He should kill him, of course. Sooner or later, most likely sooner, Morales would come back and put two and two together. With Dutchy's pickled brain but still-sharp eyes, they'd come to their conclusions even more quickly, and now that Dutchy had managed to find out about the baby, things were getting too damned dangerous. The best way to protect the baby and the woman as well, would be to kill him.

He looked at the old man. He was the scum of the earth, and he certainly had earned death many times over.

The problem was, Dutchy was right. He had grown soft. Ten years ago he wouldn't have hesitated, and Dutchy would have already breathed his last.

But he'd seen enough death, enough killing to last him the rest of his life. He was going to take his chances. If they moved fast, they'd be out of reach before Dutchy started blabbing, safely up in the deserted village of Puente del Norte, ready to fly out of the country.

Of all the places, why had he chosen Puente del Norte to land? Fate wasn't making things any easier for him, or for the woman sitting in the front of the canoe.

Reilly looked at the top of Carlie's head. The short dark hair was lightening in the sun, streaked with gold among the dark brown. He didn't know whether she'd fallen asleep, but at least she'd ceased that soft, loving murmur she directed at the baby.

The sound of her voice, her damned *nun's* voice, should have infuriated him. Indeed, it did, but it also crept under his skin and teased at him, making him horny and crazy and wanting to hit something.

He'd left the Catholic church years ago, but he still knew that a nun was off-limits. And much as he wanted to discount Dutchy, and believe the man's words were all lies, he knew he couldn't. There were too many things pointing straight at that unpalatable truth, including her total unfamiliarity with her body's sexual potential. The way she kissed. The way she looked at him. The way she walked and talked, totally without sexual guile.

At first he'd assumed it was some act of a well-bred tramp like Caterina Morrissey—a sham innocence meant to be alluring, and he'd had to admit that it was.

Knowing it was real innocence should have destroyed any random traces of lust left in him. Unfortunately, life didn't work like that.

He looked at her sun-streaked head, bowed low over the baby, and he thought about the taste of her mouth, the wetness he'd coaxed between her legs, the perfect fit of her breast against his hand. He looked at her, and he still wanted her. And nothing, not decency, not charity, not wisdom, could still the desire surging through his body

He told himself he wouldn't do it. From now on it was strictly hands off. No touching, no loaded comments, no cursing if he could help it. She'd made her choice, and he wasn't able to offer her any reasonable alternatives. They were two people, thrown together for a few days in a dangerous situation. It was no wonder his hormones were running high.

Once they made it out of here, once she was safely settled wherever the rest of her…sisters were, he'd get beyond it. He'd spend a little extra time in D.C., looking up a few old friends. His buddies were always trying to match him up, and this time he'd let them. He needed a woman, not a girl. Someone a little older, a little more experienced, should wipe away Carlie's memory in no time.

He knew when she'd fallen asleep. When her tense shoulders relaxed, her entire posture softened and a faint, watery sigh drifted back to him. She'd been crying, he realized belatedly, with a pang he quickly stifled. Why had she been crying, for God's sake? Over her imagined sins?

The sun was growing brighter overhead, and he steered the dugout closer to the riverbank and the protecting overhang of greenery. She'd already absorbed enough sun on her pale skin—he didn't want her burned. It would slow them down, he added to himself. Lying to himself.

Damn, damn, hell and damnation. And then he found he still maintained a sense of humor. For all that his cursing was uncharacteristically mild, it was all too accurate. Hell and damnation would be awaiting him, for messing with a nun.

Particularly since he still wanted to mess with her, quite badly. He wanted to finish what he had started, and he didn't want to think about white-and-black robes, and vows of chastity. He wanted to think about the look in her eyes, the scream she'd made, pressed up against his shoulder. He wanted to see whether he could make her scream again.

He reined in his imagination with steely control. She'd been trouble enough in her other incarnations. As Caterina Morrissey she was a selfish tramp who was looking for a meal ticket, as Carlie Forrest she wasn't much better. But Sister Maria Carlos was the worst of all. The sooner he was out of this mess, the better. He'd head straight to his mountaintop and stay put, and nothing, but nothing, would make him come down.

After he got thoroughly and satisfyingly laid, of course. He needed to get this particular woman out of his mind, out of his blood, out of his fantasies. And it would take another woman to do it.

Hell, he might not wait until he got to D.C. If Simeon could find someone for him, he'd take care of his little problem right then and there, and too damned bad if the holy sister didn't like it.

There was no way he was going to pretend that he was in anything else but a foul mood that day on the river. He pulled alongside the riverbank for a brief stop, made the bottle for the kid when needed and grudgingly partook of the bread and fruit the Shumi had packed for them. But he wasn't about to indulge in any social amenities, and she seemed perfectly willing to accept his disapproving silence.

Hell, she was probably used to silence, he thought bitterly. What kind of vows did they take? Chastity, he knew that one for sure, and it was a thorn in his side and his conscience. Poverty and obedience. Well, she'd flunked the last one, but if she was supposed to keep silent she was doing a good job of it.

They reached the tiny landing of Cali Nobles by late afternoon. It wasn't much larger than the small outpost where Dutchy lived, but Simeon was standing on the rickety wharf in the dying sunlight, his eyes shaded with one beefy hand, looking toward them.

"I damned well don't believe it," he bellowed heartily. "I thought you told me nothing in God's name would ever bring you back to San Pablo?"

Reilly controlled his instinctive wince. "I decided I missed your blue eyes, Simeon. Not to mention this lovely peaceful climate."

"Yeah, sure," said Simeon, grabbing the end of the boat as it drifted toward the dock and taking a good long look at the woman in the front. "And who's this? You decided to experience the joys of marriage and fatherhood after all?"

"Not me, Sim," he said, jumping from the boat and tying up the back end. "I'm too smart for that kind of trap." Carlie was struggling to her knees, and he moved to loom over her. "Simeon McCandless, let me introduce you to Carlie Forrest and her young son, Timothy."

She glanced up at him, her blue eyes wary and doubting, but she had enough sense to keep silent. It wasn't that he didn't trust Simeon—hell, he'd stake his life on Simeon's worth, and had more than once—but the fewer people who knew the truth about the baby, the better.

"Pleased to meet you, ma'am. You picked an odd time to be traveling downriver."

"It wasn't exactly a matter of choice," Reilly said in his driest voice as he reached down to help Carlie out of the boat. He hadn't wanted to touch her, but there was no way she could clamber out of that small dugout without tipping everything into the water, including the baby.

She landed on the dock beside him, lightly, the baby clasped capably in one arm. She looked like a natural mother, he thought distantly, gazing down at her. And she was a woman who'd turned her back on motherhood, and sex.

"It's nice to meet you, Mr. McCandless," she said with studious courtesy.

Simeon's laugh traveled from the base of his huge belly. He was a British expatriate who lived life on the edge of civilization, and he was one of the few men Reilly really missed from San Pablo.

"You're too good for the likes of Reilly anyway, lass," he said. "Come along to my place and we'll get you and the baby settled. I have a native woman who cooks for me, and she'll fix you up something nice and hearty while Reilly and I catch up on old times."

"It sounds lovely," she said faintly.

"Lovely it's not, but it'll do," Simeon said. "And I promise, I won't keep your man from you for too long."

"He's not my—" she started to say hotly, but Reilly interrupted her smoothly.

"She's learned to be patient, Sim. Besides, I need to hear about what sort of visitors you've been having in this area. Any of Morales's renegades been visiting? And what about the noble revolutionaries?"

"Those stupid bastards," Simeon said, spitting for emphasis. "Fortunately for them, they've kept to the west. They're too mad to keep from killing and too damned stupid to keep from killing the wrong people. Morales has been in the west as well, near Dutchy's place. You hear about Dutchy?"

"Hear what?" It was a sign of just how dangerous his companion was to his state of mind. If he hadn't been thinking about her bare feet on the dirt-packed path to Sim's house, he would have realized that probably wasn't the best question to be asking.

"Dead, old man," Sim announced. "Happened sometime last night or this morning. Single gunshot to the back of the head, I gather. Not that he's any great loss, but it does seem strange that his good buddy Morales would suddenly turn on him. Unless it wasn't Morales."

"Is that who they're saying did it?" Reilly asked in a neutral tone of voice. He could feel the tension vibrating through Carlie's body. There was no doubt that she thought he'd killed him and then lied to her.

He was only slightly tempted to shove her against the nearest wall and confront her. If she thought he was capable of cold-blooded murder, so be it. It might make her walk a little more warily around him.

It would be unlikely to encourage her to confide the truth in him, but since she didn't seem in the slightest hurry to do so in the first place, who was he to care?

"Come on, angel," he drawled, taking her arm in one strong hand. "The sooner we get to Sim's place the sooner I can have a beer." He looked down into her eyes, expecting to see rage and disgust. What he saw instead startled him. Grief, pure and simple, and a numb kind of despair.

"I have Scotch as well, Reilly," Sim said cheerfully, missing the furious undercurrents. "I remember you were always partial to a good Scotch."

"I'd like some Scotch, too," Carlie said after a moment in a strained voice.

"Of course," Sim said with perfect courtesy.

"No, you don't." Reilly overrode her. "You're too easy a drunk as it is. Two beers and you collapse. We aren't wasting good whiskey on you. Particularly when we might have to hightail it out of here without a moment's notice."

"Someone after you?" Sim questioned knowingly.

"Who isn't? If you've got a bed for the night and transportation north that's all I ask."

"Why do you want to go north? That's where most of the fighting's been during the last ten years. There's not much up there but a few burned-out villages."

I left the plane up there."

Sim nodded. They'd reached the small frame house he called home. He pounded up the steps, past the empty hammock that stretched across the sagging porch, and paused by the dim interior of the place. "I'm sure I can arrange something. For the three of you?"

He looked down at Carlie's bowed head. "Can't leave my lady behind," he said deliberately.

"I though you two weren't..."

"We're not married," Reilly said. "But we're together."

"I'm glad for you, old man," he said sincerely, heading into the house. "Just let me find us some glasses, and we'll have a toast."

Not if you know what I've landed myself with, Reilly thought ruefully. Sister Maria Carlos looked about ready to take a knife to him herself.

He was damned if he was about to start making excuses to her. He wasn't the one who lied. "You'll be staying in the room at the top of the stairs," he said. "Why don't you take the kid and make yourself scarce? I need to talk to Sim."

"You lied."

"Bull."

"You killed him. You murdered him in cold blood and then you lied to me...."

"Liars are the scum of the earth, aren't they?" he drawled. "I can't say I'm any too fond of them, either, but now isn't the time to argue about it. Just get your cute little butt upstairs and we'll talk about it when I finish with Sim."

"Finish with him? Are you going to take his Scotch and his hospitality and then kill him, too?"

"The only person I'm interested in killing right now is you," he said flatly, glaring down at her. "Now get upstairs before I take you there and give you something you'd regret even more than you regret last night."

"Bastard," she said, her voice a furious hiss. It was probably the first time she'd ever uttered that word out loud, and her eyes widened in telltale shock at her own temerity.

"Why, Sister Maria Carlos," he drawled. "Such language from a Roman Catholic nun."

For a moment he thought she'd faint. She turned a dead white beneath the soft pink color of sunlight across her cheeks, and he was ready to catch her, and the baby, if she crumpled.

But she was made of sterner stuff than that.

She didn't say a word. She simply turned her back on him, that narrow, straight back that he found so delectable, and marched up the stairs.

And not once did she look back.

Chapter Thirteen

Carlie could hear them downstairs. Talking. Laughing. She hadn't thought a man like Reilly could laugh.

She lay in the center of the wide bed, awake, listening, waiting. The baby was sound asleep in a makeshift cradle, and Carlie was half tempted to wake him up, just for the distraction. There were too many things hurtling about in her mind, not the least of which was whether Reilly was going to come up and join her in that bed.

It was a small house, she knew that. Two bedrooms—Simeon's and the one she was in. There was no other place for him to sleep, and he was hardly likely to worry about her feelings in the matter.

She ought to be able to sleep. She was exhausted from the three days of travel, from the worry, from the heat of the sun. She'd eaten well tonight, thanks to the cheerful native woman who was most likely Simeon's mistress, and she'd managed a decent sponge bath.

Reilly hadn't said a word to her since they'd arrived. Ever since he'd called her by her religious name he'd all but ignored her, leaving it up to Simeon to get her settled and fed. And even now, in the sultry heat of the jungle night, she still had no answers to her questions.

Why had he killed Dutchy and then lied about it? And how did he know the truth about her? And had he known last night, when he'd ... he'd ...

She slammed down the memory as heat suffused her body. She didn't want to think about last night. About the restless, desperate feelings he'd engendered inside her. And what he'd done to resolve those feelings.

The peace she'd fought so hard for seemed to be slipping away, and no matter how much she struggled, she couldn't bring it back. She'd been away from the others for less than a month, she'd been out of the convent for no more than seventy-two hours. And already she knew there was no going back.

At some point the voices below fell silent. At some point she slept, dozing in and out of a troubled, dream-filled sleep. She dreamed of guns and blood and sex, and when she awoke in the pitch darkness, alone, panic filled her.

She climbed out of bed, pulling a pair of cutoff jeans under the oversize white T-shirt, and looked down at Timothy. He was sleeping soundly, and Carlie blessed the fates that had given her a peaceful, noncolicky baby.

Except that he wasn't her baby. She needed to remember that—she'd be giving him up soon enough. By tomorrow they'd reach the plane, and then they'd be out of San Pablo. Reilly would take Timothy to his rich grandparents, and Carlie would go back to

Mother Ignacia. But she already knew she wouldn't go back to stay.

The night was silent, warm, and yet Carlie's skin was chilled. The dream still haunted her. Dutchy, his eyes dark and empty, blood pouring from his wounds, had held out his hands to her, begging for help.

There was no way she was going to get back to sleep without confronting Reilly. He might decide to take a gun to her, as well—so be it. If he'd killed Dutchy, then some of that guilt rested on her head. She needed to know.

She had no idea where she'd find him. There were no clocks in Simeon's house, few clocks in San Pablo, but Carlie knew well enough that it had to be around three in the morning. She crept down the narrow stairs. An empty whiskey bottle lay on its side on the rough table, two glasses, one empty, one half-filled, beside it. There was no sign of Reilly in the rough-and-tumble room.

Maybe he'd decided to abandon them after all. Or maybe he'd simply gone off with Simeon's well-endowed lady friend. She couldn't second-guess where he'd gone, and she didn't want to go too far in search of him. She could still hear the baby if he happened to wake up, as long as she went no farther than the porch.

The porch was what she needed. She picked up the half-full glass of whiskey, knowing instinctively it had been Reilly's, and took a tentative sip. It was burning, foul tasting, sending tendrils of warmth through her chilled limbs. She took another sip, wandering out onto the front porch in the moonless night.

It took her a moment to realize she wasn't alone. Reilly lay in the hammock, seemingly asleep.

She almost turned and went back inside. The idea of confronting Reilly no longer seemed quite so smart. Not when he turned her insides into a roiling mass of confusion.

But she wasn't a coward. The past three days had taught her that much. And when she moved toward the hammock she saw that his eyes were open, and he was watching her.

"I should have known I couldn't sneak up on you." She was resigned.

"You're lucky you didn't try. I might have cut your throat before I realized who you were."

The words hung heavily on the night air, and Carlie shivered once more. "Why did you lie to me?"

"About what?"

"About Dutchy. You killed him, and then you told me—"

"I didn't kill him." His voice was flat. "When I left him he was unconscious, tied to his bed but very much alive."

"I heard the gunshot."

"I'm not going to try to convince you," he snapped. "You can believe me or not. I have no reason to lie to you. I've killed before in this life, and I'll probably have to do it again. But I didn't kill Dutchy."

The realization hit her then, astonishing as it was. Reilly was offended that she didn't believe him. Even hurt. As ridiculous as it seemed, Reilly was angry that she didn't trust him.

Carlie shook her head, wondering if the small sip of whiskey she'd taken had rattled her brain. "I do trust you, Reilly," she said softly, carefully.

"I don't give a damn whether you do or not."

"Yes, you do," she said, suddenly sure of herself. "If you say you didn't kill Dutchy then I believe you."

"You didn't before."

"I do now."

"Why?"

For a moment she couldn't answer. He was lying stretched out in the old rope hammock, his feet bare, his shirt open to the night breeze, his eyes dark and derisive. He looked dangerous and very strong, and the longing that washed through her made her soul tremble.

She managed what she hoped was a cocky half smile. "Maybe because I know you wouldn't lie to a nun."

He was not amused. He stared at her for a moment, as if considering the possibilities. "Come here," he said.

She ought to go right back upstairs, she knew it. "The baby might—"

"You can hear the baby if he cries. Come here."

Her body didn't seem interested in listening to her mind. She found herself standing beside the hammock, dangerously close to him. There was a soft night breeze, and it ruffled her T-shirt, danced through her hair. "I suppose you want me to say I'm sorry I lied to you," she said nervously. "And you want to know why I entered the convent and why I didn't tell you the truth. And you probably want me to tell you that—"

"I don't want you to tell me a damned thing," he said. He reached out and took her wrist in his big hand, and pulled her into the hammock.

She was too astonished to do more than put up a token struggle. Before she realized what was happening he'd tucked her up against the warm length of his body, cradled in the comfort of the old hammock. He held her there, lightly, his arms around her, her face nestled up against his shoulder. "Now go to sleep," he said gruffly.

She lay there, frozen, astonished. She waited for his hands to move, to stroke her once more, but they remained decorously still, and his body was calm, relaxed against hers, his breathing even, his heartbeat steady against her racing one.

It was probably close to ten minutes before she accepted the fact that that was all he intended to do. Simply hold her. The realization brought a rush of relief. And a surge of shameful frustration.

She knew he wasn't asleep, despite the evenness of his breathing. He lay peacefully beside her, but his body and mind were tuned to the night, to the creatures of the darkness that were an unbidden threat to their safety. Just as his body was tuned to hers.

"You don't want to know why I joined the convent?" she said finally, in a very quiet little voice.

He didn't answer for a moment, and she wondered whether she misjudged him, and he slept. And then his hand moved, long fingers threading through her shaggy hair. "I imagine it had something to do with seeing your parents killed."

She took a sharp breath. The words were so simple, and so painful. "They were missionaries, you know. Not Catholic, but when the relief workers brought me down out of the mountains and took me to the Sisters of Benevolence, it seemed as if it were God's will that I follow in my parents' footsteps. To take their place."

"So that's what you did," he said, his voice a low rumble in his chest. His skin was warm, sleek against her cheek, and she resisted the urge to push against him like a kitten seeking pleasure. "You took their place. How long have you been there, Carlie?"

"Nine years. It's been so peaceful. I never wanted to leave. I wanted to stay with the sisters, take my final vows and never have to deal with the real world. But then the revolution came. And Caterina."

"And me," he added.

"And you." Her hand had slid under the open khaki shirt, crept up to his muscled shoulder. She could smell the tang of whiskey on his breath, mixing with the thick smell of the rain forest.

"So what are you going to do now?" he murmured. His mouth was close to her ear, and she could feel the warmth of his breath as they rocked together in the narrow hammock. She was safe enough, she thought. Despite her limited knowledge of procreation, she knew people couldn't make love in a hammock. Could they?

"I'll go back and join the others," she said, trying to ignore the fluttering in the base of her stomach, the faint, clenching feeling between her breasts. "They've gone to a convent in Brazil. When we arrive in the States I can get in touch with the nearest diocese and they'll help me. That is, if you're still willing to take me back."

"If I wasn't?" The words were even, suggesting nothing other than mild curiosity.

"Then I'd find my way there myself."

"I'll get you there," he said, his voice deep and unreadable. "Once we get the baby to his grandparents I'll make sure you end up where you should be."

That promise should have comforted her. For some reason it didn't. She let out her pent-up breath, trying to will herself to relax against him. It wasn't that she couldn't get comfortable. Reilly's body fit hers all too well.

"Just tell me one more thing, Carlie," he murmured against the side of her face. "You've been in the convent for nine years. You're how old—twenty-three? Twenty-four?"

"Twenty-six," she said.

"Then how come in all that time you haven't taken your final vows? That's what you said, isn't it? You're still an apprentice nun, right? How come you didn't graduate?" he drawled.

"I'm going to. As soon as I join up with the others," she said.

"How come you haven't already?"

She actually considered lying, astonishingly enough. The only lies she'd told so far had been to protect a helpless infant, not herself. If she were to lie now, to him, it would only be for her own selfish sake, and there was no way she could justify it.

"Reverend Mother Ignacia didn't think I was ready," she muttered, hoping he'd leave it at that.

Somehow his arm had gotten underneath her, and his hand curved around her waist, dangerously close to her breast. He wasn't touching her, but she could feel the heat and the weight of his hand on her rib cage, near her racing heart.

"Why weren't you ready?"

"She wasn't certain if I had a calling."

"Are you certain?" he murmured, his mouth against her earlobe.

She was having a little trouble breathing. "Absolutely," she said in a strangled voice, waiting for his mouth to move, to settle against hers. Waiting for the dangerously sweet oblivion he could bring her, so easily.

He didn't move. For a moment time seemed to stand still. And then his hand fell away, to rest on her hip, and his body relaxed against hers. "It's always nice to be sure about what you want in life," he said in a deliberately neutral tone of voice.

She felt his withdrawal, even as his hand claimed her hip. He was letting her go, she realized with surprise and relief. And some other strange emotion she couldn't begin to identify.

It shouldn't have surprised her. He'd slept with her, stripped her clothes halfway off her, kissed her, caressed her, and yet she still remained as virginal as the day she was born. He'd told her he simply wanted to relax her into sleep last night, and that's exactly what he'd done. He hadn't seemed the slightest bit interested in...in making love to her, any more than he did right now.

He probably simply didn't find her attractive. Or if he had, finding out she was a nun put an end to his roving lust, and for that she could thank God. Couldn't she?

"Reilly?"

"Yeah?"

"How'd you find out I was a nun?"

"Dutchy told me. He remembered where he'd seen you before. It didn't seem to bother him that he'd almost raped a nun, and I guess he thought I'd think it was pretty funny. I didn't."

"But you didn't kill him."

"Carlie..." His voice carried a very definite warning.

"I'm not asking," she said hastily.

"I wanted to kill him," he said. "I was tempted. But I decided I'd seen enough killing to last me."

"Why did you want to kill him? Why then?"

"It was a question of shooting the messenger. I didn't like what he had to tell me. I didn't want to hear you were a nun and I'd just done my level best to despoil you."

She couldn't help it—she smiled against his shoulder. "That couldn't have been your best effort," she said, nestling closer to him, her hips up against his. He seemed a mass of tight, hard bulges and muscles, and she tried to imagine the male anatomy with her limited knowledge. "I can't imagine you not succeeding at anything you set your mind to, and I'm only slightly despoiled."

"Carlie." His voice was low, warning. "Watch it."

She felt safe, secure. He didn't want her, he wouldn't hurt her, he'd take her back to the convent and this would all be a wild dream. "Watch what?" she murmured, rubbing her face against the smooth heat of his skin.

He moved so fast the hammock swung wildly as he pulled her underneath him, pushing between her legs so that she cradled him against her hips. He was hard, pulsing, alive.

"There's a limit, Sister Maria Carlos," he said in a tight voice, a deliberate reminder to both of them. "I'm a man, with a man's body and a man's needs, and if you push me you'll find out just what that involves."

She stared up at him in surprise. "Don't be ridiculous, Reilly. You don't really want me. You could have had me at any time when you thought I was Caterina, and you didn't. You..."

Her voice trailed off as he began to curse. She didn't even understand half the things he was saying, but she knew enough to know they were vile and heartfelt.

"I don't want you?" he muttered, half to himself. He took her hand in his, dragging it down between their bodies, pushing it against the straining zipper of his jeans. He was rigid, pulsing beneath her hand, and he held her there, forcibly. "If I don't want you, what the hell do you think that is?"

She looked up at him. "I've been in a convent since I was seventeen," she said quite frankly. "I don't know."

He froze as the simple truth of her words penetrated. And then he cursed again, but this time the words were directed at himself, as he released her hand from his iron grip.

She didn't move it. He felt strange to her fingers, hard and mesmerizing beneath the thick denim and the heavy zipper, and she traced her fingertips against the length of him, curious.

He yanked her hand away, shoving it against the hammock, and the look in his face as he loomed over her was full of fury and something else she wasn't ready to comprehend. "That's an erection, Sister Maria Carlos. It means I want you, so badly that it's tearing me apart. It also means I'm not quite the bad guy I like to think I am, because I'm not going to take you. I'm going to send you back to the Reverend Mother in the exact same shape I got you. If you want to experiment with sex you'll have to find someone else to cooperate."

"I don't want to experiment with sex," she said in a muffled voice, aware of the deep color flooding her face. Aware that she wanted to reach down and touch him again through the thick material. She kept her hands to herself.

"Just as well. Virgins are a bore, and a hammock's for the more advanced," he drawled, his fury seemingly gone. A mask of cynicism had fallen over his face.

"What makes you think I'm a virgin?" she said hotly.

"It's a fairly simple deduction. If the soldiers who wiped out that village had found you, you wouldn't be alive. Since you've been in a convent since you were seventeen and you've never even heard of an erection, I imagine you're probably the oldest living virgin left in San Pablo. Am I right?"

"You're a bastard."

"We've already agreed on that. Are you a virgin?"

"Yes, damn it."

"I don't know, Sister Maria Carlos. If your language keeps going the way it has been, the Reverend Mother might not let you back into your safe little hiding place."

Safe little hiding place. That was exactly what Mother Ignacia had told her. She was hiding from life.

She tried to pull away, but he held her tight, his long fingers wrapped around her wrists. "I'm going upstairs to bed," she said furiously.

"No, you're not. You're staying right here, with me. We'll sleep in peaceful, celibate bliss," he snapped.

"Why?"

"Let's just say I believe in suffering the torments of the damned," he replied, shoving her face against his shoulder.

She lay there fuming. She lay there plotting revenge, escape, anything she could think of. She lay there tucked against his big, strong body, his smooth skin, and she wanted to cry.

Somewhere in the distance she could hear the sound of gunfire. Far enough away not to be a danger. The sky was growing light—they'd been arguing for hours. She closed her eyes, unutterably weary and sick of the battle. She could feel the warmth of his breath against her hair. The soft brush of his lips against her temple, but she knew it had to be her imagination. Reilly wouldn't want to kiss her. He wanted to be rid of her, just as much as she wanted to get away from him. Didn't she?

She sighed, letting her lips drift against the warm column of his throat, feeling his pulse beneath her mouth. Heavy, strong, hypnotic. She wanted to stay like this forever, safe in his arms, listening to the steady beat of his heart. As long as he held her, she was safe.

HE'D BEEN TOO HARD ON HER, and he knew it, Reilly thought as he felt her relax into a dreamless sleep. She'd been through so much in the past few days—it was no wonder she was confused. It wasn't her fault that her infuriating combination of unawakened sexuality and courage ignited some impossible longing deep inside him.

It was sex, pure and simple, he tried to tell himself.
He wanted to get between her legs, and knowing she
was forbidden made him want her even more.

He wasn't going to have her, but it wasn't her fault.
He could probably talk her into it—she was vulnerable, she was grateful when she wasn't fighting him,
and she was attracted to him, whether she knew it or
not.

He could have her, and he'd be damned if he did.
Literally.

Chapter Fourteen

The sound of the noisy engine dragged Carlie from her sound sleep, and she awoke, startled, alone, swinging back and forth in the old hammock.

It was daylight, and Reilly had left her. It was only to be expected. By tonight they'd be out of the country, perhaps even out of each other's company. Ready to go their separate ways.

She scrambled out of the hammock, wincing as her bare feet landed on the rough pine flooring, and leaned over the railing to look at the vehicle that had just driven up. The old truck had seen better days. Better decades, Carlie thought as Simeon jumped down from the driver's seat. It took three attempts to get the driver's door shut, and the passenger side was held together with chicken wire.

"What do you think?" Simeon surveyed the decrepit old truck with a misplaced satisfaction.

"This will take us to the airfield?" she asked doubtfully. "There doesn't look like room for the three of us."

"There isn't," Reilly said, appearing in the doorway of the ramshackle house. He was shirtless, with a day's growth of beard on his jaw, and he held the baby against him with a natural grace. Timothy was awake, looking up at him out of those somber brown eyes, waving one tiny fist. "You and the kid are riding in back."

"Without a baby carrier and a seat belt? No," she protested, moving to take the baby from him.

Reilly made no move to relinquish him into her waiting arms. "Listen, angel, Morales and his men are between us and the deserted village where I left the plane. You're more likely to get a bullet in your brain if you sit up front with me, and then what the hell good would a seat belt do? You'll be hidden down behind some boxes, and I won't need to worry about anyone but me being a sitting target if we have to make a run for it."

"Are we going to run into them?"

"God knows. I don't. So far we've been fairly lucky, but sooner or later our luck is going to run out."

She reached out again. "I'll take the baby."

"No, you won't. He and I are getting acquainted."

She dropped her hands, tucking them around her body, feeling oddly bereft. They made a cozy picture, the big, strong man and the little baby, both shirtless, both male, both gorgeous. A family picture, and she was excluded, on the outside, looking in.

It was her choice, she reminded herself. Her destiny. She'd have to relinquish both of them soon enough—she may as well get used to it.

"Fine," she said with a bright, false smile. "I'll get the rest of our things from the room."

"I already brought them down while you were sleeping," he said brusquely. "The baby's fed and changed, and everything's set to go. As soon as you're ready we can take off."

She squashed down the feeling of guilt that accompanied her odd sense of bereavement. "All right," she said in a deceptively tranquil voice. "Obviously you can manage perfectly well without me."

"I don't see that we're going to have much choice in the matter."

"Children, children," Simeon said smoothly. "There's no need to squabble. Let me get you some of my best coffee, Carlie, while Reilly plays make-believe daddy. Maybe it'll convince him that marriage and children aren't such a dismal prospect."

"They're not a dismal prospect," Reilly said, moving out onto the porch in the early-morning breeze and settling into the hammock with Timothy clasped safely against his chest. "They're just not for me."

Simeon's bearded face creased in a smile. "So you say. We'll see whether it ends up that way."

She followed Simeon into the marginally cooler interior of the house, determined not to look behind her. To notice that there would have been room for her on that hammock as well, to curl up next to Reilly and the baby.

"So how do you like your coffee, Carlie?" Simeon asked, handing her a mug. "Black as night, sweet as sin, strong as love?"

"I hadn't thought of it that way," she said faintly, taking a deep, grateful gulp of the brew.

"No, I imagine you haven't," Simeon agreed innocently.

Carlie glanced up at him. "He told you."

"That you were a nun? Yes. I think he wanted to make sure I behaved myself. Not that Reilly seems to be making much of an effort," he added easily, lowering his impressive bulk to a rickety-looking chair.

"He doesn't like me."

Simeon frowned. "You don't believe that any more than I do, child. He may not approve of your life choices, but the problem is he likes you far too much. I never thought I'd see Reilly succumb."

"Succumb to what?" she said, curiosity getting the better of her wariness.

"To the fair sex. To family values. To love, child."

"Don't be ridiculous!" she snapped.

"I've known Reilly for more than ten years. I've seen him with lovers and enemies, friends and acquaintances, and during all that time I've never seen him look at a woman the way he looks at you. For what it's worth, I think it scares the hell out of him."

Carlie drained her coffee, failing to savor it. "I think," she said carefully, politely, "that you've been out here a little too long."

"Denial is not just a river in Egypt."

"I beg your pardon?" she said, mystified.

"That's right, he said you've been immured in a convent for the last decade. It means, child, that you're lying to me, but more important, you're lying to yourself." He waved an airy hand. "Go ahead, though. I won't argue with you. It's between you and Reilly. When the time comes for you to go back to your sisterhood, will you go? Or will you stay with Reilly and the child?"

"You don't understand," she said miserably. "We'll all go our separate ways, alone. Timothy will go to live with his grandparents, Reilly will go back to wherever he comes from, and I'll join the sisters."

"Colorado," Simeon said.

"I beg your pardon?"

"Reilly lives on a mountaintop in Colorado, in a house he built himself. He lives alone."

"He probably prefers it that way."

"So he says."

"And I'll be very happy to be back with the sisters," she said firmly.

"And you're sure that's what you really want?"

There was amazing kindness in Simeon's eyes, and she wanted to tell him the truth. She wanted to put her head in his lap and weep out her confusion and doubt. The frightening truth of her feelings for Reilly, feelings she didn't want to have. The convent was no longer home for her. But what home did she have?

Reilly had appeared in the door behind her, silent, but his shadow blocked out the early-morning sunlight. "It's what I really want," she said firmly.

Adding another lie to her list of sins.

THE PROBLEM WAS, Reilly thought as he pulled away from Simeon's place, that she didn't look like a nun. Part of the problem was Caterina Morrissey's clothes. Those skimpy shorts, exposing a surprising length of leg for such a small creature, the lack of bra beneath the T-shirts, the short-cropped hair and the defiant eyes added up to a potent, tempting package of womanhood. If she was dressed in veils, with her eyes modestly downcast and her language demure, he could keep himself in line. But every time he glanced at her, at her pale mouth and wary eyes, her lean, luscious body, he wanted her.

At least he didn't need to glance at her now. She was comfortably settled in the back of the truck. Timothy lay strapped in a makeshift bassinet, and there were several layers of blankets protecting her from the rusted floor of the old vehicle. It wasn't the safest arrangement, but safety was a relative issue in San Pablo these days. He just needed to get them through enemy lines, back up into the mountain village where he'd left the plane, and they'd be home free.

He knew his way around the northern forests. He'd been stationed just over the border, in Costa Rica, for two years back in the eighties, and during that time his platoon had spent the majority of their days and nights roaming through San Pablo. Back then he had been busy trying to make the world free for democracy. That was before he'd learned that one man's democracy was another man's fascism, and that all governments were screwed up.

It was almost over. By tonight, or tomorrow morning at the latest, they'd be back in the U.S. Sister Mary Charles would be back to the bosom of her convent, the baby would be on his way to D.C., and he could put all this behind him. Just four days of tropical madness. Four days of falling for the one person he couldn't have.

She'd been tempted, though. She might not know the signs, but he certainly did. The way her bones softened when he touched her, and her eyes glazed over. She wanted him almost as much as he wanted her.

Of course, he was about to take care of that. Once she found out where they were actually headed she wasn't going to feel the slightest bit lustful. She was more likely to be downright murderous.

Hell, it wasn't his fault where he'd decided to land the plane. Just simple bad luck. There were few enough places in the sparsely populated mountains of San Pablo, and the only logical place to land a small plane was the burned-out remains of an old village. One that had seen a massacre just nine years before.

She wasn't going to like returning to Puente del Norte. For the past two days, ever since she'd told him the truth, he'd been racking his brains for another way out.

There wasn't one. She was going to have to return to the place where she'd watched her parents being slaughtered. And she wasn't going to like it. And she wasn't going to like him for taking her there.

Problem solved. So why didn't he feel just a little bit more cheerful about the prospect?

CARLIE WAS surprisingly comfortable in the back of the pickup truck. The canvas covering flapped in the wind, cooling her as they rumbled along, the baby slept and she didn't have to look at Reilly.

Which was definitely a mixed blessing. She liked looking at Reilly—liked it too much. It was just her luck that after being shut away from the majority of the opposite sex, she got thrown together with what was undoubtedly a prime specimen. It didn't require a great deal of experience to know a handsome man when she saw one. And Reilly was most definitely a handsome man, in his own, unbending way.

She was going to have to get used to not looking at him. Today was simply good practice.

The road was narrow, rutted, climbing through the jungle, higher and higher through the sultry, green-canopied forest. The smells were different here—different, and yet oddly familiar. Carlie glanced out past the flapping canvas, but all she could see were the endless, dark depths of the forest as they climbed higher.

It started with nothing more than a simple gnawing in the pit of her stomach. She knew it wasn't hunger, or sickness. She'd eaten enough of the simple food Simeon had packed for them, and she should have been content to doze on the pile of blankets, next to the baby.

But something was wrong. Something was terribly wrong. It began to spread through her body, a miasma, a sense of disaster, of a horror so great, a terror so deep she would never climb out of that bottomless hole. She knew where they were going.

She knew it from the grim expression on Reilly's face when they'd stopped earlier, and the way he'd refused to meet her gaze. She knew it from the pounding of her heart, the cold sweat that covered her, the trembling that started slowly and then grew more and more overwhelming.

She lost track of time. Hours, days, years passed as the truck rattled up the steep incline, an incline she knew too well. She knew when it would level off, and it did.

She told herself she might be wrong. Why would fate, and Reilly, have brought her back to this place of death? She tried to lift her hand, to move the canvas away to reassure herself that she'd been mistaken, but her hand lay motionless in her lap, paralyzed.

Timothy began to whimper. Just quiet little sounds as he stirred from his sleep. Carlie wanted to murmur something soothing, but her voice was trapped behind her mouth. She heard the whimper turn into a cry of protest, and she knew he needed her. Needed to be changed, needed a bottle, needed her arms around him.

She couldn't move. She couldn't go to him, comfort him, see to him. She sat, huddled against the side of the truck as it bounced along, listening as the cries turned to angry wails as he lay there, trapped, abandoned, and she couldn't help him, all she could do was curl up in a little ball, shaking, terrified, panting so loudly they might hear her, they might find her, they might do to her what they'd done to her mother and the girls of the village, while their screams echoed in her ears as she hid, she hid, and the blood was everywhere, and it was death, and pain, and she couldn't help him, couldn't go to him, couldn't go to them, couldn't . . .

"Carlie!"

She heard him calling her, but she wasn't sure whose voice it was. Her father, calling for help, calling her to run away and hide. Or Reilly.

She curled up tighter, her hands over her ears, trying to shut out their cries, the baby, her parents, the people of the village, the laughter and shouts of the soldiers, the gunfire, the gunfire . . .

REILLY WORKED FAST, efficiently, despite the uncharacteristic panic that filled him. The moment he heard the baby's wails a chill washed over him, and he ditched the truck in a copse just outside the village.

He just had time to see Carlie, curled up in a fetal ball, before he dealt with Timothy, stripping the sodden diaper from him, propping the hastily made bottle of formula in his hungry mouth before he could turn to Carlie and pull her into his arms.

She probably had no idea who he was, but it didn't matter. She needed someone to hold her, to murmur soothing words, to hold her so tightly the monsters in her memory abandoned her. She was icy cold, sweating in the thick heat of the jungle, her breathing was rapid and shallow, and her eyes were unseeing. He cursed himself inwardly, all the while keeping up a soothing litany of comforting nonsense. He should have found some other way out of the country, despite the risk. For now, all he could do was cradle her rigid body in his arms and try to warm her.

"The baby..." she managed to gasp through deep, shuddering breaths, her fingers digging into his arms as she tried to drag herself back.

Reilly glanced over at him. "He's fine. I gave him a bottle, and he's asleep again."

"I couldn't...help him...." The words were coming in hiccups as she shivered helplessly. "I couldn't save him."

"He's fine," Reilly said again. "Just take deep breaths, Carlie. It's over. It's in the past. No matter how bad it was, it's gone."

"They're screaming..." she gasped.

"No. It's over, long ago. No one's hurting anymore. They're at peace now. Except for you."

It jarred her. She jerked her head up to look at him out of bleak, desperate eyes. "Make it go away, Reilly," she whispered.

He knew what she wanted. Oblivion, life. She wanted the one thing from him he'd been determined not to give her.

"No," he said as gently as he could, ignoring the need that swept through his own body. He couldn't do it to her. She was lost, broken, hurting. She needed comfort. Not a further betrayal.

"Please," she said, begging, her hands gripping his shirt. "Please."

And he knew that he was going to take her. He was going to deflower a nun in the back of a pickup truck, with a sleeping infant beside them. And nothing, either in heaven or hell, could stop him, no matter what the consequences.

Putting his mouth against hers broke the last of the spell. She kissed him back, desperately, as she pulled his shirt away from him.

Stilling her restless hands with one of his, he slowed the kiss, using his tongue, kissing her with a leisurely thoroughness that stole her terrified breath. He could feel the warmth begin to seep back into her flesh, feel the restless stirring in her limbs.

"Please," she said one more time when he lifted his head to look down at her.

"All right," he said, hating himself. "But we'll do it my way. Slowly. So there won't be any mistakes. So you know what you're doing, and you won't change your mind."

She wasn't listening to him. She wasn't interested in noble motives, she wanted oblivion. As he did.

He skimmed the T-shirt over her head, baring her breasts, half hoping to shock her into a latent sense of self-preservation. She made no effort to cover herself, and he realized it was he who needed preserving.

She simply stared up at him, mute, pleading, and with a muffled curse he gave up his last attempt at decency.

He'd tried. God only knew, he'd tried to resist her. But now it was too late, and things had escalated beyond his control. He needed her, and the sweet death her body and soul could provide him, almost more than she needed him.

CARLIE LAY BACK on the rough wool blankets, lost. His hard, deft hands pulled her shorts off, tossing them away, and she was naked, vulnerable, as he leaned over her, darkness and longing in his eyes.

She was beyond rational thought, of sin or redemption, past or future. All that mattered was now. All that mattered was that he touch her, kiss her, take her. Now.

His hands covered her breasts, gentle, rough-skinned, and she closed her eyes, arching against his touch. His mouth followed, catching the tiny nub and suckling like a baby, his long hair flowing down around her.

She reached up to touch him, to pull him closer, and felt the frustrating barrier of his khaki shirt. She pushed at it, and it was gone, and his skin was smooth and warm against hers.

She felt no fear, for the first time in years. Just an overwhelming sense of rightness, of need. His hands, his mouth were everywhere, seducing her when she had no need to be seduced, filling her with a sense of power and delight.

He kissed her breasts, her stomach, her hips. He put his mouth between her legs, as he'd promised and warned her, and she cried out, feeling her body convulse immediately, darkness prickling against her eyes.

And then he moved up, lying between her legs, cradled against her hips, and she could feel the rough denim of his jeans.

"We'll stop now," he whispered in a tight voice. "You can— "

"No!" She caught his narrow hips with desperate, angry hands, clawing at the denim. She bucked against him, stray tremors still flashing through her body, as she tried to edge closer, to crawl inside his skin, to take him, to make him take her.

"Carlie." His voice was almost desperate now, but she was beyond rational thought. "I can't do this to you."

"You can't stop," she said, reaching between them for the zipper of his jeans.

It was tight over his erection, and her hands were awkward, hasty. He stopped her desperate fumbling, unfastened his jeans and shoved them out of the way.

He was hot and hard and heavy against her, but she wasn't going to let him stop. "Now," she whispered. "Please."

He cupped her face with his hands, looking down at her, as he slowly began to fill her. His face was taut with tension and he was big, huge, pushing into her. She knew a moment's panic, that it wasn't going to work, that he was going to pull away and leave her like this.

"Relax," he whispered against her mouth. He started to withdraw, and she clutched at him, desperate.

"Don't leave," she cried in a broken voice.

"I can't," he said, his voice full of despair and triumph. "Take a deep breath."

She did so, automatically, but before she could release it he'd pushed against her, breaking through the frail barrier of her innocence, filling her.

She screamed, more in shock than actual pain, but his hand was already against her mouth, muffling the sound.

She closed her eyes. She could feel the dampness of tears seeping down her cheeks. "That's enough," she said in a strangled voice. "I'm satisfied."

"No," he said shortly. "You're not." And he began to move, pushing into her, his hands cupping her hips and pulling her up to meet his strong, steady thrusts.

She struggled, for one brief moment. And then she clung to him tightly, and it took her only a heartbeat to catch his rhythm.

It all began to fall away—the jungle, the stillness around them. Her body was sick with sweat, and his was, too. He put his mouth against hers, kissing her hard, and she kissed him back, her legs coming up to wrap around his hips, her breath sobbing in her lungs, as she reached for the darkness once more, the endless oblivion she craved.

It hit her, fast and furious, but it was no oblivion. He was with her all the way, his body rigid in her arms as he pushed in deep and filled her with the pulsing heat of life and death.

She wept then, clinging to him, pulling him tightly against her as the spasms racked her body. She could hear his breath rasping in her ear, the shudders rippling through his big, slick body. He collapsed on top of her, his heart banging against hers, and she trembled, holding tightly, as errant waves of reaction scattered through her.

It seemed as if everything she knew, everything she believed had been shattered by his hands, his mouth, his body. She felt adrift, helpless, floating on a dangerous sea with no land in sight, nothing to cling to but the strong, tough body covering hers.

But he would disappear, as well. At any moment she'd be alone again, as she had been for so very long. His breathing slowed, and she wondered whether he'd fall asleep. The women who came to the mission, bringing their children for Carlie to teach, would joke about their husbands when they thought Sister Mary Charles wouldn't hear.

What would they think if they saw her now?

She waited for the shame and misery to wash over her. They didn't come. Despite everything, there was a tiny burst of joy bubbling inside of her. And she knew that no matter what happened, she could never regret what she'd done. What she'd shared. Who she loved.

Reilly, it seemed, was a different matter. He began to curse, low in his throat, a tapestry of foul language that would have made her blush a few short days ago.

He pulled away from her abruptly, and she let him go, knowing that she couldn't hold him.

He yanked his jeans up, still swearing, then bounded off the back of the truck without looking at her.

So much for romance, she thought. She was wet between her legs, and blood stained her thighs. She'd have to wash, but for now it took all her energy to pull the big T-shirt over her head and wrap it around her body.

Timothy slept. The bottle had fallen to one side, drained, and she squashed the vision of guilt that danced through her mind. He would survive. They all would.

She leaned her head against the truck, weariness fighting with her odd exhilaration. She couldn't hear any trace of Reilly, and for a moment she wondered if he'd abandoned them.

She quickly discarded that notion. He wouldn't have brought them so far, only to leave them.

He'd return, sooner or later. In the meantime, all she could do was wait.

And remember the feel of his body against hers, and the sure, undeniable knowledge that she loved him.

Chapter Fifteen

This day, thought Reilly, had definitely gone from bad to worse. He'd just deflowered a nun in the back of a pickup truck, then abandoned her, cursing a blue streak. By the time he'd walked to the edge of the burned-out village street and realized she might need...something, it was too late. He'd come face-to-face once more with none other than former general Endor Córdoba Morales. Better known as the Butcher of La Mensa.

Morales was alone this time, which was a small blessing. He was also armed to the teeth and pointing a particularly nasty Luger directly at Reilly's gut. "I thought you might turn up sooner or later," he said pleasantly. "Though I must admit I thought you'd be a little better prepared. Didn't you realize we'd catch up with you?"

It didn't help, Reilly thought grimly, that he was shirtless and unarmed. And that he was scared to death that Carlie might take it into her head to follow him.

"We passed your men about ten miles down the mountain," he said with deceptive calm. "How come you're alone?"

"I wouldn't worry about it, Reilly," Morales said pleasantly. "I can handle an ex-soldier like you and the little nun without any help."

Hearing his name didn't help Reilly's pessimism; neither did the fact that Morales knew who Carlie was. "I assume Dutchy was the one who filled you in on those little details."

"Dutchy was a very useful man when his head wasn't clouded with liquor."

"Then why did you kill him?"

Morales shrugged. "My wretched temper," he said with a disarming smile. "When I heard he'd let you get away, I'm afraid I reacted...hastily. Where's your little friend, the good sister?"

He didn't bother denying Carlie's identity. "I left her downriver. She was heading for La Mensa—she wanted to rejoin her convent."

Morales's smile broadened, exposing blackened teeth. He was an ugly man, with a pitted face, a short, stocky body and dark, tiny eyes radiating malice. "No," he said. "You just came from her—I know the look. You have scratch marks on your chest. The good sister must be a real tigress. Where is she?"

"I told you—"

"Don't anger me," Morales said. "It's been a while since I've had a nun," he added in a musing voice. "I like being the first, but then, she's prettier than most of the nuns I've raped. Tell me, Reilly, was she willing?"

"She's on her way to La Mensa," he said again.

"And did she take *el presidente*'s grandson with her?"

He didn't even flinch. "I don't know what the hell you're talking about."

"I must say, you impress me," Morales murmured. "Cool as a cucumber, don't they say? I will admit, part of the reason I killed Dutchy was that I was angry with myself. I didn't realize you were attempting to ferry the last Mendino out of San Pablo when you arrived at Dos Libros. If I had, I could have saved myself some time and trouble. And my men would have enjoyed Sister Maria Carlos." He shrugged, and the gun never wavered. "They will get their chance, though. They're off looking for you. I don't know how you missed passing them when you made your way up here."

"I know how to keep a low profile."

Morales frowned. "My men are the best."

"They're not good enough."

Morales considered the notion, the light of cruel madness dancing in his eyes. "Apparently not. Get on your knees, Reilly."

"Why?"

"Because you're too damned tall, like most yanquis. If you want to die fast and painlessly you'll get on your knees so that I can reach the back of your neck."

Reilly just looked down at the little pip-squeak. "I'm not going to die on my knees," he said calmly.

"I can shoot you in the eye, then. It'll take longer, but you'll be just as dead." Morales cocked the pistol. "Where are the nun and the baby?"

"There's no baby, and I left the nun outside of Dos Libros," he said stubbornly. There was a shadow moving behind the burned-out shell of the nearby building, and he hoped to God it was something bigger than a rat. A jaguar, perhaps, looking for a tasty military treat. Though if he got a sniff of Morales's pungent odor he might have the good sense to run in the opposite direction.

There was nothing Reilly could do. Morales was too far away; if he dived for him he'd have a bullet in his brain before his feet left the ground. It just went to prove what he'd always known—once he started thinking below the belt he was doomed.

Lust confused a man, at least temporarily. Love killed him. Facing his own imminent death, he considered the possibility of love, something he'd managed to avoid in all his sexual relationships. It seemed to have crept up on him when he wasn't looking.

"I'll have to kill the nun as well, of course," Morales continued. "Though chances are my men will see to that—they're not very civilized, and few whores have survived their combined attentions. But there's the question of the baby. I can't afford to let a member of the Mendino family survive. He could disrupt my own plans. Should I feed him to the crocodiles? Or perhaps just leave him here, alone, for the jungle cats to find?''

"There is no baby," Reilly said stubbornly.

Morales fired the gun.

It hit him in the shoulder, spinning him around and knocking him to the ground. Morales moved to stand over him, an ugly smile on his ugly face. "I'll go for the knees next," he said. "I can keep it up for quite a while, until you tell me what I want to know. I'm certain you know I'm enjoying this. It's up to you. You can deprive me of my fun and make it easier on yourself. Or we'll do it my way."

"There is no baby."

Morales cocked the pistol again and aimed it at Reilly's zipper. "Then again, there are other places we can start."

Reilly didn't flinch. "There is no baby," he said again.

And in the distance, floating toward them from the hidden pickup truck, came the unmistakable sound of a baby crying.

Morales jerked his head around, momentarily startled, though the gun never wavered. Reilly coiled his muscles, ready to kick at him, when the figure emerged from the shadows. Carlie.

Morales whirled around, but he wasn't fast enough. She had a huge section of burnt timber in her hand, and she sent it crashing down against his head with all her might.

He went down like a felled tree, and the gun scattered in the dust of the deserted village. He lay there, dazed, panting, as Carlie stood over him.

He started to rise, reaching for one of the guns tucked into his waistband. Carlie crossed herself, muttering something and whacked him again. This time Morales stayed down.

She looked across his fallen body to Reilly. To the blood streaming down his arm, soaking into his shirt, and he half expected her to faint.

She didn't. "Have you got a first-aid kit?" she demanded. "I can take care of that for you."

He shook his head, wondering if he'd imagined the past few minutes. "It's just a flesh wound," he said, struggling to his feet, the blood running hotly down his arm.

"I know that," she said calmly. "I've had medical training—I've dealt with far worse."

He believed her. He believed her capable of anything.

"In the plane," he said. "It's just beyond the end of the street."

Her eyes closed for just a moment of pain. "Near the graveyard," she said.

"Yes."

She nodded, and he could see the visible effort it cost her. She looked down at Morales's comatose figure. "Is he alone?"

"For now. His men will be here soon enough."

"Then we'd better get out of here, hadn't we?"

"I'll get the baby."

"You're wounded...."

"As you said, it's just a flesh wound," Reilly said. "You've seen worse, I've had worse. I'll get the kid. Keep an eye on Morales. If he moves, mash him again. Though I expect I don't need to tell you that."

"No," she said. "You don't."

SHE WATCHED HIM GO, steeling herself not to panic at the sight of his blood. She knew it was only a slight wound, but the sight of it still tore at her. This wasn't a stranger's blood, a stranger's gunshot wound. It was Reilly. The man she loved.

He disappeared into the greenery, and a moment later Timothy's howling stopped. He was a good man, Carlie thought. A good father. He was just what the baby needed.

She looked down at the evil creature lying in the dust. She hadn't killed him, though she almost wished she had. It hadn't been him that day, nine years ago, but he was part of the whole evil society that lived on blood and killing.

She lifted her head and looked down the street. It looked so different, and yet the same. The houses were burned to the ground, and the jungle was encroaching. No one lived here, no one had come to take over the abandoned lands. The place was haunted.

She knew where the cemetery was. Where the plane would be waiting. Down at the end of that narrow road.

She was still barefoot, as she had been most of the two years that she'd lived there. The dust caked her feet, and she remembered the blood that had pooled there. She looked ahead, down toward the plane, and saw that she wasn't alone.

They were there, all of them. The ghosts of Puente del Norte, watching her.

For one brief moment she wanted to run away and hide. Back to that secluded spot where she'd huddled behind a tree and tried to blot out the screams. The place where they'd found her, days later, numb with shock and horror.

But she held her ground. There was nothing to be frightened of. There was her best friend, Maria, smiling at her, red ribbons in her thick black hair, a fiesta dress swirling around her bare ankles. And Maria's parents, Amana, who'd been a second mother to her, and Carlos, the patriarch of the village, the stern, strong man who'd been the first to die.

They looked happy to see her. Smiling at her, waving to her as she started down the empty road.

Her parents were there, as well. Slightly distracted, as they always had been, more concerned with the well-being of mankind than the well-being of one small child, they nevertheless looked at her with love and pride.

It's not your fault, they said with their eyes. *We're glad you survived. That you lived. You live for all of us. Forever.*

She walked. Past friends and family, the old medicine man, the babies, the children and the ancients. Past their smiles and nods and love. And when she reached the end of the village path, and there were no more ghosts, she turned to look at them.

They were fading now. Almost into nothingness, and she realized she was letting them go. At last.

"Goodbye," she whispered. Barely the breath of a sound.

Goodbye, they called to her. And they were gone.

REILLY'S SHOULDER HURT like bloody hell. He'd flown one-armed before, in shock, and he'd managed to land the plane safely. He had no doubt whatsoever he could do it again, particularly since Carlie had managed to bandage the flesh wound with surprising dexterity.

He couldn't take any pain pills, though, and for that he was grateful. The constant throbbing in his shoulder kept him alert through the long hours of night flight. And it helped keep his mind off Carlie, asleep beside him.

But nothing could keep him distracted forever. Not when she was so close, her newly tanned legs stretched out beside his in the small cockpit. She'd be covering up those legs soon enough, draping them in long robes. It was wrong, he thought. Wrong that those beautiful legs would be covered. Wrong that her maternal love would be stifled. Wrong that she'd never lie in a man's arms again.

And most wrong that she'd never lie in his arms again.

He was flying into Hobby Airport in Texas, the closest, safest place for them to land. Wait Morrissey would be seeing to the paperwork, getting them

cleared through customs, arranging for a proper birth
certificate for his grandson. Would he mind not having a daughter-in-law? Probably not—it made the
balance of power simpler. And Wait Morrissey was
definitely into power.

He glanced over at Carlie. She was dozing, the lights
from the instrument panel reflecting on her pale face.
She looked tired and infinitely sad. He probably
looked like hell himself.

But the baby sleeping in her arms appeared peaceful and healthy. He looked as if he'd gained weight
over the past few days, while they'd fought for their
lives. Kids were resilient, he'd always been told. Well,
Timothy Morrissey was proof of it.

He was going to miss him. It was an odd notion—he
loved his nieces and nephews, but he'd never felt the
particular lack in his own life. He did now. The past
four days, with the three of them forced together into
their own nuclear family, had had a disturbing effect
on him. All his carefully formed ideas about who and
what he was, and what he needed in this life, had been
shot to hell.

He'd do the right thing, of course. He'd give Timothy to his wealthy, powerful grandparents, he'd send
Carlie back to the safety of her convent and he'd go
home to Colorado, back to his mountaintop, alone. At
peace.

Like hell. Peace wasn't going to have anything to do
with it. It was going to be utter hell for the next few
weeks. Maybe even a month or two. But sooner or

later he'd forget her. Forget the kid. Get on with his life.

It was a good thing he'd already gotten out of this game. He could have killed them all, thinking with his hormones instead of his brain. He hadn't expected Morales to have separated from his men, but survival depended on expecting the unexpected. If it hadn't been for Carlie he'd be lying in a pool of his own blood, his extremities shot away. And God knows what would have happened to Carlie and the baby.

He shuddered, unable to help himself. He was too damned vulnerable, and he hated it. He needed to get rid of them, as soon as he could. And maybe then he'd return to normal.

Wait Morrissey had already done his part. It was three in the morning when Reilly approached Hobby Airport, and all it required to get landing clearance was Morrissey's name. Everything was taken care of, Major Reilly. Even hotel rooms.

Carlie barely roused when they landed. She took her return to her native soil with an odd diffidence, following silently behind him, the baby clasped in her arms.

Morrissey had booked them into a two-bedroom suite with all the amenities. It was past five and already growing light when Carlie settled the baby down in the portable crib. And then she looked over at Reilly, standing in the bedroom door.

"You need to get that shoulder looked at," she said.

"Why? You did a good enough job. I'll have someone take a glance at it when I get back to Colorado."

"Is that where you live?"

"Yes."

The silence was taut, nervous. "Do you want anything to eat?" he asked suddenly. "I was going to call room service."

She shook her head. "I think I'll just take a shower and sleep. When are we taking Timothy to his grandparents?"

"Wait Morrissey is coming here to get him. I have no doubt that someone informed him the moment our plane landed. We'll see him late this afternoon, I believe."

Her face looked stricken. "What about his grandmother? I wanted to see where he'd be living, I wanted..."

"He'll be fine, Carlie."

She took a deep, steadying breath. "Of course he will."

He didn't move. "Are you all right?" he asked abruptly.

She jerked her head up, and there was a faint wash of color on her pale face. "Why wouldn't I be?"

It was a challenge, but cowardice was one crime he had yet to commit. "You lost your virginity a few hours ago," he said calmly. "I wondered if you were feeling all right."

"Just peachy."

There was nothing he could say. She'd pulled a wall around herself, a brittle defense he could probably smash if he cared to. He didn't. She needed all the protection she could get. Particularly since he was about to withdraw his own.

"All right," he said, backing out of the room. "I'll see you later."

"Yes," she said. But it sounded like goodbye.

IT HAD BEEN SO LONG, Carlie thought. She wasn't used to this place. To the cleanliness, the elegance, the sheer size of everything. The bathroom was larger than some houses in San Pablo, and it came equipped with enough towels for a family of four, and a basket full of little bottles of sweet-smelling soaps and unguents.

The shower had endless hot water. A good thing, because she stood in there letting the years, the pain, the sorrow wash away from her, she stood until she almost fell asleep, with the water sluicing over her, washing San Pablo, washing the blood, washing the sex away.

She had sinned. In so many, many ways. She had hit a man, twice, instead of turning the other cheek. For all she knew he might be dead, and even worse than committing that crime, she didn't regret it.

She was awash with covetousness. She didn't want this luxury surrounding her, but she wanted warm showers and shampoo. She wanted a comfortable bed and enough food.

She had lied, to Reilly, and to herself. She had lied about who she was, she had lied about what she wanted.

She had sinned. She had lain with a man, she had kissed him and she had made love with him, and she wasn't sorry. She wasn't shamed, or repentant. She was defiantly, gloriously glad she had done it, and she was half-crazy with the burning desire to do it again. And again. And again.

It would be a mistake, she reminded herself when she finally turned off the still-warm shower. He didn't care about her, and he was about to abandon her. Most likely he would make love to her if she demanded, but it would mean nothing to him. And it would only tie her heart more closely to him.

She was going to have to release them, both the baby and the man. The two creatures she loved far too much, and she had no claim to. It was time she started letting go.

The hotel room came equipped with thick terry-cloth robes. She pulled one around her, then went and lay down on the bed in the twilight gloom, listening to the deep, even breathing of the sleeping child.

There was no noise from the adjoining room. Reilly must be sound asleep. Superhuman he might seem, but the past few days of running, little sleep, topped off with being shot, had to have taken their toll on him. He was probably dead to the world.

Whereas she had slept too much—on the plane, in the back of the truck. She'd slept enough to last her for quite a while—she wasn't going to sleep away the last few hours she had with Reilly and the baby.

It took her a moment to realize the odd feelings shimmering beneath her breastbone. She was happy. For the first time in nine years she was free, of the guilt, the horror, the memory. She was free of the past, with its pain and despair. She was free of the present, with its rules and repressions.

She was free of the future. It would be lonely, empty, without Reilly and the baby. But she'd survive. She'd survived so much already.

But for this brief moment she was blissfully, gloriously free.

And even if it hurt her more, made it even harder to get on with life, she wasn't going to waste this moment.

She'd made love with Reilly in despair and pain and panic, rough and quick in the back of a truck with death all around them. She was going to make love to Reilly in a huge bed, with clean white sheets and all the time in the world. The sin was committed, and she didn't regret it. Now she needed something to help her through the long empty years.

There would be no other man for her, she knew it with absolute certainty. There would be no other babies for her.

What she would have would be a perfect memory. And it would have to be enough.

Chapter Sixteen

He lay stretched out on the huge bed, his strong, tanned arms outflung, the white sheet covering his hips. She had no doubt he was naked underneath it. She moved to the bed, silent, unsure of herself, knowing this was foolish and wrong and terribly, terribly right.

He was lying on his stomach, his face turned away from her, covered with a long fall of dark hair. But as she stood there his hand lifted and caught hers, and he turned to gaze at her, his eyes dark and gleaming in the murky light.

He looked absolutely beautiful lying there, tanned skin against the white sheets, staring up at her. He'd shaved the rough stubble of beard, and it made him look oddly civilized, elegant, despite the long hair and the scarred, wounded body. "Are you sure, Carlie?" he said, his voice a low promise of desire. "There are no excuses this time."

"No excuses," she said, turning her hand to catch his, palm to palm.

He rolled onto his back, reaching up to unfasten the loose belted tie of the robe, so that it fell open. And then he tugged her, gently, down onto the bed, pushing the terry cloth off her shoulders, holding her against him, carefully, tenderly, as he kissed her mouth.

It was a wonder of a kiss, sweet and searing, a promise of long dark nights and lazy afternoons. A false promise, she knew that, but she didn't care. All that mattered was now.

He rolled her over onto her back, leaning above her. "We'll take it slow this time," he murmured against her mouth. "We need to find out what you like. What you don't like. What frightens you." He bit her earlobe, gently.

"I don't know much about men's bodies," she said, feeling awkward and shy.

He smiled a gentle smile, free from mockery. "You can learn," he said. "What do you want?"

"I want you," she said, breathless, honest.

"You have me," he replied, the solemn words a kind of vow. "You can do anything you want. Nothing is forbidden." He leaned back, watching her, waiting.

She came up on her knees beside him, wondering where to start. She put her hands on his chest, on the smooth, warm skin, tracing the line of his ribs, the old scars, the definition of his musculature. She leaned over and kissed his throat, her tongue flicking out to taste the clean, soapy taste of him. He made a quiet growl that sounded like approval, and she moved her mouth downward, across his chest, kissing, tasting, biting.

His hands were on her shoulders, gentle, encouraging but not forcing, his long fingers kneading her pliant flesh, as she reached his flat belly, and the barrier of the white sheet.

She hesitated for only a moment. And then she pulled the sheet away, tossing it toward the end of the bed.

He wanted her, though she'd had no real doubt of that. He wanted her very badly indeed. And yet he made no move to take her, to force her, to hurry and control her, simply giving her free access to his big, strong body that had protected her so well, loved her so well.

She touched him, letting her fingers curl gently around the silken length of him. Once more it astonished her that she could accommodate him, but he'd already proved that she could. She would again.

He seemed to swell and grow beneath her touch, even though she wouldn't have thought it possible. She skimmed her fingers down the shaft, and he made a strangled sound in the back of his throat, almost like the purr of a man-eating tiger.

She slid her fingers down, to cup him, and his muffled word was more a prayer than a curse.

She stroked him, gently, amazed at the pleasure it gave her, as well. She was growing hotter, shakier, as she touched him, learned him.

The purr turned to a growl as he reached up and caught her hand, pressing it down over him, increasing the pressure, showing her the rhythm and force he wanted, until he arched his head back with a groan.

Nothing is forbidden, he'd told her. And with pure instinct she leaned down and put her mouth where her hand had been.

He gasped her name and caught her head between his hands. She could feel the tension thrumming through his body as he tried to control his reaction, the strength in his hands as he tried to gentle his touch.

It astonished her—his powerful response to her experimental caresses. But what amazed her even more were her own emotions. She was trembling with arousal, needing him, lost in a dark maze of delight and desire until she no longer knew what she was doing.

She was barely aware of him moving. He lifted her off him gently, turning her to lie on the bed. She was shivering with longing, and she tried to pull him over, onto her, but he resisted easily.

"Your turn now," he said in a rough voice, but his hands and mouth were gentle as they danced across her skin.

She heard her quiet whimper from a distance, and she reached for him blindly, frightened, needing him. It was so strange and distant, this fear and trust, entwined around her like a vine, capturing her, so that all she could do was lie back and revel in the terrifying wonder of his hands on her body as he brought her to the screaming edge of completion.

He came to her then, stretching over her, resting between her legs. She braced herself, but she was slick and damp, and his thrust filled her, deep and full and glorious.

She arched against him, lifting her hips to draw him deeper still. "Hold on," he whispered in her ear. And then he flipped over, taking her with him, so that she was on top of him, his body still tight within hers.

For a moment she panicked. But he simply arched his hips, thrusting up into her, showing her the rhythm, his big hands holding her hips, moving her in delicious counterpoint.

"That's right," he murmured, his voice a tight whisper of sound. "Take me, angel. Any way you want me."

She learned it, so quickly. She arched, flinging her head back, as she sank down on him, and she felt powerful, splendid, magical. She moved with perfect, erotic grace, reveling in the tension of his body beneath hers, the sweat-slick skin, the fierce, glazed look in his eyes.

She felt it start, a shimmering tension that threatened to shake her apart, and suddenly she lost the smooth rhythm she'd mastered and began to weep. Not knowing why, awash in emotions and feelings and fear she couldn't begin to understand. "I can't," she cried, but he simply took over, turning her once more so that she lay back against the mattress, fingers clutching the sheets.

"You can," he said, low in her ear. And he reached between their bodies and touched her.

It hit her with the force of a hurricane. Blackness clamped down over her as her body convulsed. She heard him, felt him come with her, and she clung to him as tightly as she could, riding the storm.

It seemed an eternity before she opened her eyes. She knew he was watching her. He lay beside her, holding her close, but there was no hiding from his searching gaze. She opened her eyes and met it.

He looked somber, troubled. His long hair fell loose about his face, and his eyes were haunted.

"Don't look so guilty," she said with an attempt at lightness. "I'm the one who came to you."

"Carlie," he said, but she reached up and covered his mouth with her hand, her fingers stroking the firm contour of his lips.

"It's all right, Reilly," she said. "The sin is mine, if that's what you're worried about. Though I expect you don't even believe in sin. But it's my sin, not yours. I just wanted to...wanted to..." Words failed her, and she dropped her head.

"Wanted to what?"

"To see what it could be like," she said in an apologetic voice. "When it's done out of love."

"Carlie..." he began, his voice dangerous.

"Don't worry about it, Reilly. I know you don't love me. That's perfectly understandable. I'm someone you were saddled with while you were trying to repay an old debt. But you see, like it or not, I love you. And I really believe that anything done in love isn't a sin."

Timothy set off a distant wail, and she slid out of bed instantly. Reilly grabbed for her, but she was already out of reach. "We haven't finished talking," he said, his voice rich with anger and frustration.

"Yes, we have." She paused by the door. "There's nothing more to say. I love you and the baby, and you don't love me. Don't make it harder for me, Reilly. I know how you feel. Just let me deal with losing both of you in my own way."

And she ran from the room before he could stop her.

REILLY LAY BACK and began to curse. He knew curses in a dozen languages, though he usually preferred Anglo-Saxon words. His second favorite were Arabic curses, and he let go with a few choice ones, aimed directly at himself.

It was her damned fault as well, he thought furiously. She hadn't given him a chance to say a word, to even think about things. The past few days had been so crazy, it was no wonder he was absolutely out of his mind. The worst thing he could do was make some stupid, impulsive gesture that he'd wind up regretting for the rest of his life.

It wasn't as if she didn't have a place to go to. He could count on Wait Morrissey to see her safely back to wherever she wanted to be, and if Morrissey dropped the ball, then he'd damned well hand-deliver her to her precious Mother Superior.

Of course, she'd be in slightly shopworn condition. And the thought of facing some stern old nun scared him more than seeing Endor Morales on the empty streets of Puente del Norte.

But she'd made her decision, clearly. This was best for all of them. They'd all go their separate ways, and it would give him time to think. To consider. To plan.

Except that he wasn't that kind of man. He made snap judgments, spur-of-the-moment decisions, and he lived with the consequences. His instincts were almost infallible, and they'd kept him alive for more than fifteen years in some of the world's most dangerous places.

His instincts were telling him he'd be a fool to let her go.

He climbed out of bed, in a thoroughly bad mood that his satisfied body didn't seem to share. He wanted to go after her, to grab her and shake some sense into her. Why didn't she make demands, demands he could give in to? Why was she making this so damned difficult?

He needed breathing space, and so did she. He'd give her time to think things through. A couple of hours for her to consider the alternatives. And then he'd go in search of her and inquire very politely whether she might be interested in spending a little time in Colorado. To see whether the climate might suit her.

He was just coming out into the living room of the suite when he heard the knocking. Maybe Carlie had ordered room service. Then again, maybe she hadn't. The door to the other bedroom was still tightly shut, and there was no sign of her or the baby.

For a brief moment he wondered whether she'd run. Taking the kid with her. He wouldn't blame her, but he didn't think it was likely. Sister Maria Carlos had a bit too much honor to take that route. Even if her heart was breaking.

The pounding on the door continued, and he strode toward it, yanking it open. "Yeah?" he snarled.

"Reilly!" Wait Morrissey stood there, glowering at him, looking so damned much like Billy that Reilly wanted to punch him.

"Wait," Reilly said in his most noncommittal voice, blocking the door. "We weren't expecting you till later."

"We have an important cocktail party tonight, so Gracie insisted I charter a plane and get here early. She would have come with me but there were too many last-minute details she had to take care of. She's hired a lovely Mexican gal. Doesn't speak a word of English, but then, neither will my grandson at this point. Where is he, Reilly?"

"Here." Carlie's voice came from directly behind him, and Reilly had no choice but to move out of the way and let the old man in. He didn't want to. He wanted to tell Wait Morrissey to go to hell and take his wife with him, but he clamped his jaw down.

Wait was staring at Carlie with undisguised doubt. "You're not Caterina Morrissey," he said in an accusing voice. "What the hell's going on here, Reilly?"

"I'm Carlie Forrest," she said. "Caterina was my friend."

"Was?" Wait echoed. "She's dead?"

"I'm afraid so. She died in childbirth."

Morrissey bore down on Carlie. He was an impressive man, bulky, powerful, with the ability to intimidate most people despite the overbearing charm he wielded like a weapon. Billy had been scared spitless of him, and even Reilly watched his step.

Carlie didn't move. "So you got Reilly to give you a free ride out of the country at my expense," Wait said. "Well, forget it. You're responsible for any extra passengers you pick up along the way. I'll take care of any debts my grandson incurred."

"I told you, I don't need any money," Reilly snapped, but Wait ignored him, staring down at the baby.

"We can sort that out later," he said grandly. "I take care of my own. Assuming he even is my grandson."

Timothy didn't like the sound of the old man's voice. Reilly didn't blame him. The baby let out a loud, furious wail, the likes of which Reilly hadn't heard in the past four days, his little face turning red with temper.

"What do you mean by that?" Carlie asked calmly over the noise of the screeching kid.

"I mean we're going to have tests done. Reilly should have made that clear. He's going straight into the hospital so that they can check him out, run some DNA samples, that kind of stuff. I want to make sure he's in good shape before we take him. And I want to make damned sure he really is my grandson."

"And if he's not?" Reilly said in a deceptively polite voice.

"If he's not? Well, there's no way in hell I'm raising some bastard as my grandson. And you can kiss your expenses goodbye." Wait Morrissey took a deep, calming breath. "No offense intended, Reilly. I know you wouldn't try to pawn off some brat as Billy's. But who's to say this girl's telling you the truth?"

Reilly tilted his head sideways, considering him. "No way I'd do that, Wait. Which is why I hate to tell you, but he's not your grandson."

Fortunately his simple words drew all of Wait's attention, and he didn't notice Carlie's shocked expression. She tried to say something, but Timothy's wails drowned out her attempt, and Wait wheeled around, storming away from them, already dismissing them.

"What the hell are you talking about, Reilly? What are you trying to pull?"

"Absolutely nothing. Caterina died in childbirth, and so did the baby. By the time I got to the mission the only person there was Carlie. She'd given birth a couple of weeks before Caterina, but she hadn't been strong enough to be evacuated with the others. I was there, I had the baby supplies. I brought her out with me."

"I'm not paying for it," Morrissey said instantly.

"I don't expect you to."

"Can't you shut that brat up?" The old man snarled back at Carlie. "I can't hear myself think."

"You don't need to think, Wait. I'm sorry it worked out this way, but there's nothing to be done. Just tell Gracie what happened. I think she'll manage to survive." He tried to keep the wryness out of his voice.

Gracie Morrissey wouldn't have let an infant grandson interfere with her social life, and she certainly wasn't going to let the loss of one she'd never even seen affect her.

For a long moment Wait just looked at him. For all his bluster, he was an intelligent man. He looked at Reilly, then glanced back toward the baby and the woman holding him so protectively.

"All right," he said suddenly, nodding. "It's probably just as well. Gracie and I weren't very good parents the first time around, and we're too old to change our ways. It'll work out better this way."

Reilly simply nodded, unwilling to say anything. Wait turned and walked back to the howling child, staring down at him. "Gracie'll be relieved," he muttered underneath his breath. He reached out one stubby, perfectly manicured finger and touched the baby's red face. "Have a good life, kid."

THE DOOR CLOSED behind him, and suddenly Timothy was still, a hiccupy little breath at odds with his tremulous smile.

"Such a noisy baby," Carlie whispered at him, holding him tightly. "I don't think you liked that old man very much, did you?"

Reilly crossed the room and took the baby from her arms, and she had no choice but to let him go. "He's going back to bed. He needs to start getting on a normal schedule."

"Babies don't have normal schedules," she protested.

"Well, we can try."

She looked up at him, startled. *We,* she thought, shocked. She wanted to say something, but he'd already carried the baby into the bedroom, settling him back down in the crib.

Timothy set up a tired screech of protest. "Forget it, kid," Reilly said, rubbing his back with a rhythmic pattern. "You need to sleep, and your ma and I need to talk."

She shouldn't have told him she loved him. For all his bluster, Reilly was an honorable man. He probably thought he had to make some grand sacrifice for her sake. Well, she wasn't about to let him, and she would tell him so. As soon as she got her courage together.

He looked at her over the sleeping baby. "Showdown time," he said quietly.

She followed him into the living room of the suite. "You lied to that old man," she said.

He turned to look at her. They were standing just a foot apart. She was afraid he might touch her. Afraid that if he did, she'd never want him to let her go. She couldn't do that to him.

"He's smarter than he looks. He guessed the truth," Reilly said.

"Don't be ridiculous. He wouldn't have gone off and left his grandson with you...."

"That's exactly what he'd do. I doubt they would have done any better a job with him than they would have with Billy, and Billy, God love him, was royally screwed up. No, it's better this way."

"Living a lie?"

"I thought you said something wasn't a sin if it was done in love."

"Don't!" she said, feeling mortification wash over her as she held up a hand in protest.

He caught her hand, drawing her closer to him. "He's your son, Carlie. He always has been. You know that, deep in your heart." She wanted to pull away, but she couldn't. "What do you think of Colorado?"

"Reilly," she said, "I can't let you do this. I can't make you change your life, take on a couple of lost souls because you're too decent a human being to—"

Reilly began to curse again, his usual litany of obscenity that she'd begun to find oddly comforting. "You can't make me do a damned thing I don't want to do," he growled, hauling her up against him with enough force for her to know he meant it. "I'm a reasonable man. I consider alternatives, I think about things and then I make up my mind. And you're coming with me to Colorado, we're getting married and Timothy will be ours."

"No, Reilly. I can't..."

He caught her face in his hands, glaring down at her. "Listen, I've spent the last fifteen years of my life with no home, no family, no life. Now I've got Billy's kid, and I can raise him a damned sight better than anyone else can. And I've got you. And I'm not going to let you go."

"Why not?" Her voice was low, shaky. She already knew the answer. She could see it in his eyes, in his face, hear it in his voice. But she had to have the words.

"Because I love you, goddamn it," he said irritably. "And don't you dare give me any more crap about going away. I don't care whether you believe me or not—"

"I do," she said.

"You do what?"

She smiled up at him, a glorious, sunny smile. "I believe you. And the only place I'm going is Colorado, with you and our son."

He stared down at her for a moment in disbelief. "I thought you were going to put up more of a fight," he said.

"I only fight the battles I want to win," she said simply.

He kissed her then. A long, slow, sweet kiss, of promises and forever. And then he threw back his head and laughed. "We're going to make a hell of a family," he said. "A soldier, a nun and a baby."

"Ex-soldier," she said, resting her head against his chest and listening to his steady, strong heartbeat. "A not-quite nun. And babies grow up awfully fast."

He looked down at her, and there was toughness and tenderness in his smile. "Then we'll have to make some more."

"Yes," she said, against his heart. "Yes."

Epilogue

Three Years Later

Carlie sat curled up in the window seat, staring through the frosty panes of glass to the swirling snow beyond. Winter in the Colorado mountains seemed to go on forever, and she never tired of it. Even trapped in the house with a total of five kids, and one more on the way, with her husband off on some mysterious errand, she managed to still her anxiety at the way the snow was piling up and pay attention to the child curled up beside her, her hand resting trustingly in hers.

"Ma-a-a-a." Timothy managed to put half a dozen syllables into her name as he stormed through the huge, untidy living room, his three-year-old face flushed with tears. "Trina bit me."

"Caterina!" Carlie called out in the stern voice she'd been forced to master. A moment later two-year-old Caterina Reilly toddled out of the kitchen, a deceptively angelic expression on her face.

"Took my G. I. Joe," Trina announced with an air of infinite reasonableness.

"It was my action figure," Timothy shouted back in a fury.

"Wouldn't you guys rather play something nice and passive?" Carlie inquired, knowing the question was more rhetorical than practical.

"No, Ma," six-year-old Luis replied from his spot on the braided rug in front of the fire. "You know they're hellions."

Elena stirred beside her, murmuring a protest in Spanish. She and her brother, Rafael, were the latest additions to their ménage, two preschool-age orphans from Brazil, sent northward with Mother Ignacia's blessing. Luis had been the second member of their family, arriving at their mountain cabin when Timothy had just turned one, a shy, defensive four-year-old who'd gradually accepted the love and safety they offered him. Caterina arrived next, on a snowy night like this, when Carlie had gone into labor and Reilly had barely had time to get her down to the hospital, with both kids riding along in the pickup truck, listening to Reilly's panicked cursing with awe and delight.

Then came Rafael and Elena, ten months ago. It had taken them a little longer to adjust—they'd seen too much in their short lives to trust easily. But Elena had learned to snuggle, and Rafael had discovered that Luis was a soul mate. Together they kept their young siblings in line, and they both worshiped their father.

And now there was the huge, uncomfortable, much-anticipated creature doing its best to reshape Carlie's liver. She had two months to go—the baby wasn't due till April—but she was becoming increasingly aware that this baby wasn't going to wait. This time they'd need the four-wheel-drive van to take the children along to the hospital. And this time she wasn't about to let Reilly videotape the delivery and then drag it out when friends made the trek up Paradise Mountain.

The tears that had become increasingly common as her pregnancy progressed burned in her eyes, and she fought them back with an effort. She needed Reilly, she needed his strong arms around her, she needed his deep voice soothing her.

"Where's Papa?" Elena removed her thumb from her mouth long enough to ask.

Carlie brushed her hair away from her dark, worried face. "I'm not sure, angel. But you know your father—he always gets back. We can count on him."

Elena nodded, sticking her thumb back in her mouth and curling up beside Carlie, her head resting against the bulge of her new sibling.

She could hear the noise of a four-wheel-drive vehicle in the darkness beyond the cabin, but she couldn't be sure whether it was Reilly or the snowplow. She forced herself to remain still. The children needed her calm, composed, and fear never helped anyone.

She just wished she knew where the hell Reilly had gone.

He'd just up and left, three days ago, putting down his tools in the midst of turning the loft into additional bedrooms, and he hadn't told her where he was going. He'd simply kissed her, hard, on the mouth, told her he'd be back as soon as he could, and then disappeared, before she could demand a few answers.

He'd gotten better about giving answers in the past three years. It had taken a while, but he'd learned to talk to her, to laugh with her. On the rare occasions when she let her temper disintegrate, he knew just how to charm her out of her fury. When his own temper shook the rafters, she was equally adept at soothing him.

He was going to have his work cut out for him when he got home this time. She told herself she didn't mind his going—he doubtless had a very good reason and he'd be back as soon as he could. She just didn't like not knowing those reasons. Not when her back hurt, the baby seemed more like an octopus than a baby and each wild limb seemed to be wearing tap shoes. And she couldn't stop crying.

She could see the headlights now, through the blinding snow, coming closer. Too close together for the town plow. It looked like Reilly's pickup truck, and she breathed a sigh of relief.

"Is it Papa?" Elena roused herself, her beautiful dark eyes lighting up with delight.

"I expect so." Carlie slid off the window seat, carefully, and was rewarded with a fresh kick from her burgeoning offspring. She started toward the door, but the children were ahead of her, flinging it open, letting the wind and snow swirl inside.

Carlie leaned against the wall, one hand bracing her back, not even bothering to suggest the children calm down and close the door. They were too excited.

Indeed, she had a hard time turning her own expression into a suitably disapproving one. Moments later Reilly filled the doorway, his long dark hair thick with snow, his long arms outstretched to catch all five bodies as they hurtled into his arms. Above the shrieks of delight he met her stern gaze with a rueful expression.

"Miss me?" he mouthed at her above the din.

She tried to summon up a suitable snarl, but she found herself grinning instead. "Where were you this time?" she demanded.

"I brought you something."

"Oh, God," she said in a resigned voice. "How many this time?"

"Three," he said, looking suitably sheepish. "Two cousins, Matteo and Carlos, but they're only temporary. They're on their way to their family in Washington State, but they need to stay with us for a couple of months until their parents get settled."

She looked past her husband to the three small figures in the doorway. She could see the two children, dark faced, wary, eyeing the melee with tentative interest. The person standing behind them wasn't much taller, but the parka obscured the face and body.

"Welcome, Matteo and Carlos," Carlie said, crossing over to them. They looked willing enough, so she gave them a hug, one they returned.

And then she looked at the snow-covered figure beyond them. "And who is this, Reilly?"

The third visitor pushed back the fur-lined hood, exposing a lined, wrinkled little face, dark, sassy eyes and beaklike nose beneath the plain black veil. "Motherhood suits you, Sister Maria Carlos," Reverend Mother Ignacia announced.

"Oh, my God," Carlie gasped, then clapped a restrictive hand over her mouth.

"Don't worry. After listening to your husband drive through a blizzard I imagine I've heard most curses known to man," Reverend Mother said briskly, folding Carlie into her arms. "I've come for a visit. Being the mother of the year is all well and good, but you've got another baby coming, and I need a vacation. I'm here to make sure you're taking proper care of yourself until after the baby arrives."

"Reverend Mother..." she said brokenly.

"Reilly," the old lady said in her bossiest voice, "take your wife into the bedroom and give her a backrub. I'm going to teach these children how to make fajitas."

Before Carlie could protest she found herself swept away, Reilly's strong arm around her as he pulled her into their bedroom and shut the door firmly behind him.

A relative, peaceful silence ensued. Carlie looked up, way up at him. "How did you know?" she murmured.

"That you were going crazy?" he replied, pulling her into his arms and resting a big hand on her rounded belly. "You forget, I know you pretty well by this point. There's nothing wrong with being overwhelmed occasionally. You're not a saint, Carlie, even if you sometimes wish you were."

"But they need me," she cried, leaning her head against his shoulder. "And I need them."

"And you're wonderful with them. You just need a little breathing space before Megatron makes his appearance." He stroked her belly possessively.

"Her appearance," she said.

"Besides," he said, "there's someone else who needs you around here."

She smiled up at him, leaning into his tough, strong body. "You've got me," she whispered.

"Reverend Mother Ignacia's staying for two months," he whispered in her ear. "I don't suppose there's any chance we can get Gargantua to make an appearance in the next week or two so that you and I might have a night or two of raunchy sex before we have to be parents again?"

"Maybe," she said. She looked up at him with sudden worry. "Are there too many children for you?"

He shook his head. "Nope. I could handle a few more than we've got already. What about you? Did you plan on turning into the Waltons in such a short time?"

She smiled up at him. "We can handle it," she said. "You'll just need to keep adding to the house. And I'm afraid a little sooner than you think."

For a moment a look of blank horror crossed his face. "You don't mean ... ?"

"Yup," she said. "I figure we have maybe an hour to get down to the hospital. Think you can do it?"

He began to curse, and she put her hand over his mouth with a giggle that turned into a moan and then back into a giggle again.

"You've got a nun out there, soldier," she hissed with mock disapproval.

"I've got a knocked-up nun in labor in here and there's a g.d. blizzard out there," he roared in outrage. "Let's go!"

He scooped her ungainly figure up in his arms and kicked open the door. Mother Ignacia was presiding over the horde of children in the kitchen, and Reilly paused in the doorway as Carlie grabbed for her parka. "We're going to the hospital," he announced.

"You always were an efficient child," Mother Ignacia said approvingly. "Go with God."

"And drive like hell," Reilly muttered under his breath.

They made it to the hospital in time. By six o'clock the next morning, Forrest Reilly made his appearance, weighing five pounds three ounces, followed, most unexpectedly, by his sister Ignacia, who was a portly five pounds eight ounces. Once they managed to revive Reilly from his dead faint, he looked down at his wife's exhausted expression with a glazed one of his own.

"Did you know?"

She shook her head, looking down at the babies nestled in her arms. "Reilly," she said with a faint grin, "you'd better buy more diapers."

He leaned down and kissed her, hard and deep. She kissed him back, somewhere summoning the energy to arch her back to reach him. "I love you, Reilly," she murmured.

He cupped her face. "I love you, too, Sister Maria Carlos," he said. And the snow-swept Colorado night slipped away into a glorious, white-glazed dawn. And all was peaceful.

For another four and a half minutes.

Once in a while, there's a story so special, a story so unusual,
that your pulse races, your blood rushes. We call this

TO HEAVEN AND BACK is one such book.

Danny Johnson doesn't know a good thing when he sees it.
Callie Moran is the perfect woman for him, but after losing his
fiancée a year ago, he can't look another beautiful woman in
the eye. Some celestial intervention is called for, and Jason and
Sabrina are just the pair to do it. Don't miss this companion to
HEAVEN KNOWS.

TO HEAVEN AND BACK
by
Tracy Hughes

Available in April, wherever Harlequin books are sold.
Watch for more Heartbeat stories, coming your way soon!

HARLEQUIN

AMERICAN ◆ ROMANCE®

In Name Only

With the advent of spring, American Romance is pleased to be presenting three exciting couples, each with their own unique reasons for needing a new beginning...for needing to enter into a marriage of convenience.

Meet the reluctant newlyweds in:

#580 MARRIAGE, INCORPORATED
Debbie Rawlins
April 1995

#583 THE RUNAWAY BRIDE
Jacqueline Diamond
May 1995

#587 A SHOTGUN WEDDING
Cathy Gillen Thacker
June 1995

Find out why some couples marry first...and learn to love later. Watch for the upcoming In Name Only promotion.

HARLEQUIN®
AMERICAN ◆ ROMANCE®

IS BRINGING
YOU A BABY BOOM!

NEW ARRIVALS

We're expecting! Over this spring, from March through May, three very special Harlequin American Romance authors invite you to read about three equally special heroines—all of whom are on a nine-month adventure! We expect each soon-to-be mom will find the man of her dreams—and a daddy in the bargain!

So don't miss the next title:

> #579 WHO'S THE DADDY?
> by Judy Christenberry
> April 1995

Look for the New Arrivals logo—and please help us welcome our new arrivals!

NA-1R

Harlequin invites you to the most
romantic wedding of the season.

Rope the cowboy of your dreams in
Marry Me, Cowboy!

A collection of 4 brand-new stories,
celebrating weddings, written by:

New York Times bestselling author

JANET DAILEY

and favorite authors

Margaret Way
Anne McAllister
Susan Fox

Be sure not to miss Marry Me, Cowboy!
coming this April

 HARLEQUIN®

MMC

Fifty red-blooded, white-hot, true-blue hunks
from every State in the Union!

Look for MEN MADE IN AMERICA! Written by some
of our most popular authors, these stories feature some
of the strongest, sexiest men, each from a different state
in the union!

Two titles available every month at your favorite
retail outlet.

In March, look for:

UNEASY ALLIANCE by Jayne Ann Krentz (Oregon)
TOO NEAR THE FIRE by Lindsay McKenna (Ohio)

In April, look for:

FOR THE LOVE OF MIKE by Candace Schuler (Texas)
THE DEVLIN DARE by Cathy Thacker (Virginia)

You won't be able to resist MEN MADE IN AMERICA!

Bestselling Author

Janice Kaiser

Look in on the secret lives and loves of a powerful family in

Private SINS

Brett— the brilliant young attorney who dares to fall in love with her husband's son.

Amory—a supreme court judge who will have to put his heart and life on the line.

Elliot—a man trapped by his contempt for his wife and his forbidden love for his father's bride.

Monica—the bitter wife who will make her husband pay for daring to love another.

Harrison—a senator whose scandalous affairs may cost him more than his career.

Megan—the senator's aide and mistress, whose dreams may be on the cutting block.

Get to know them intimately this March,
at your favorite retail outlet.

MIRA The brightest star in women's fiction

MJKPS

HARLEQUIN®

Don't miss these Harlequin favorites by some of our most distinguished authors!
And now, you can receive a discount by ordering two or more titles!

HT#25577	WILD LIKE THE WIND by Janice Kaiser	$2.99	☐
HT#25589	THE RETURN OF CAINE O'HALLORAN by JoAnn Ross	$2.99	☐
HP#11626	THE SEDUCTION STAKES by Lindsay Armstrong	$2.99	☐
HP#11647	GIVE A MAN A BAD NAME by Roberta Leigh	$2.99	☐
HR#03293	THE MAN WHO CAME FOR CHRISTMAS by Bethany Campbell	$2.89	☐
HR#03308	RELATIVE VALUES by Jessica Steele	$2.89	☐
SR#70589	CANDY KISSES by Muriel Jensen	$3.50	☐
SR#70598	WEDDING INVITATION by Marisa Carroll	$3.50 U.S. $3.99 CAN.	☐
HI#22230	CACHE POOR by Margaret St. George	$2.99	☐
HAR#16515	NO ROOM AT THE INN by Linda Randall Wisdom	$3.50	☐
HAR#16520	THE ADVENTURESS by M.J. Rodgers	$3.50	☐
HS#28795	PIECES OF SKY by Marianne Willman	$3.99	☐
HS#28824	A WARRIOR'S WAY by Margaret Moore	$3.99 U.S. $4.50 CAN.	☐

(limited quantities available on certain titles)

	AMOUNT	$
DEDUCT:	10% DISCOUNT FOR 2+ BOOKS	$
ADD:	POSTAGE & HANDLING	$
	($1.00 for one book, 50¢ for each additional)	
	APPLICABLE TAXES*	$_____
	TOTAL PAYABLE	$_____
	(check or money order—please do not send cash)	

To order, complete this form and send it, along with a check or money order for the total above, payable to Harlequin Books, to: **In the U.S.**: 3010 Walden Avenue, P.O. Box 9047, Buffalo, NY 14269-9047; **In Canada**: P.O. Box 613, Fort Erie, Ontario, L2A 5X3.

Name:_____

Address:_____ City:_____

State/Prov.:_____ Zip/Postal Code:_____

*New York residents remit applicable sales taxes.
Canadian residents remit applicable GST and provincial taxes.

HBACK-JM2